# *A LOVE STORY*

## "Written in the Stars"

Written By

*Ann Ra*

# About the Author

Love, oh glorious love! It is a journey that takes us to the heights of ecstasy and fills our souls with boundless joy. I wrote this love story to indulge you with the experience of unconditional sacred love in a divine union, and if it invokes euphoric feelings and makes you smile, the story is a success. Being in my own twin flame relationship is beautiful and intense, with many lessons to learn. A love I had never known existed until I experienced it myself. A love of transformation.

When we truly connect with our twin flame, the energies of love flow through every fiber of our being, capturing us in a dance of passion and serenity. In these precious moments, we can truly feel the sweetness of love enveloping us, igniting a fire within that burns with a radiant warmth. As we immerse ourselves in this divine connection, I invite the reader to join in on this enchanting voyage into the realm of pure bliss, where only love exists and where every heart beats in unison, creating a symphony of love that resonates throughout the universe. Let us embark on this journey together and bask in the sheer beauty of love, for it is a gift that brings smiles and an everlasting glow to our souls.

We are in a significant shift where humanity will transition into the higher frequencies of being. The divine purpose of Twin Flames is to assist humanity in this transition by setting an example of their sacred, holy, divine, unconditional love union.

Love is the most powerful force that transcends boundaries and brings immense joy.

There is only love; there can be no other way.

# ABOUT THE BOOK

In the celestial tapestry of destiny, a remarkable love story unfolds. "A Love Story, Written in the Stars" invites you to embark on a sacred union journey entwined with the lives of Twin Flames, Grace and Michael. Their yearning for one another, an irresistible force that defies logic and transcends traditional notions of love, acts as a magnetic pull throughout the cosmos, drawing them inexorably closer to one another. These two souls once united as one, now traverse separate paths, guided by the profound power of self-love and self-discovery.

As their destinies intertwine, the very fabric of the universe dances to a celestial symphony, heralding the divine union they were destined to embody. Through this captivating tale, I intend to ignite a flame of awareness, illuminating the profound and transformative love within Twin Flames, a grand reflection of the divine love that binds us all.

# Contents


Chapter 1.................................................................1

Introduction

Chapter 2...............................................................11

DF and DM Awakening

"The Spirit of the Divine Feminine and Masculine Awakening"

Chapter 3...............................................................20

The Search Within

Chapter 4...............................................................27

Twin Flames Reunion

Chapter 5...............................................................44

The Enchanted Evening

Chapter 6...............................................................57

Kundalini Awakening

Chapter 7...............................................................69

The Sacred Proposal

Chapter 8...............................................................80

Divine Purpose

Chapter 9...............................................................91

Uniting for a Cause

Chapter 10...........................................................101

Breaking Ground

Chapter 11...........................................................113

Amazing Grace

Conclusion..........................................................127

# Chapter 1
# Introduction

In the ever-evolving landscape of modern times, humanity finds itself at a crossroads, yearning for something beyond the materialistic pursuits that have long defined our existence. As the world becomes increasingly interconnected and complex, there is a growing recognition of the need for a spiritual revolution—a profound shift in consciousness that transcends religious dogmas and embraces a broader, more inclusive understanding of our interconnectedness. In this exploration, we will delve into the concept of the spiritual revolution and its relevance in shaping our lives and society today through the experience of unconditional love and this topic swirling around this Twin Flames love story written in the stars.

Understanding the spiritual revolution and the sacred purpose, Twin Flames are here for a grand purpose: to assist in humanity's transition into the golden age of Aquarius. At its core, assisting humanity's spiritual evolution represents a profound awakening in human consciousness, a collective call to transcend the limitations of the ego-driven, materialistic paradigm that has dominated our world. It is an inner journey of self-discovery and transformation, driven by the quest for meaning, purpose, and a deeper connection to the world around us. This holy opportunity transcends religious boundaries, emphasizing the universal aspects of spirituality that can be found in various traditions and philosophies.

Relevance of humanity's spiritual revolution is seeking meaning and purpose: In an era marked by superficiality and constant distractions, spiritual evolution allows individuals to explore their inner landscape and heal, seeking deeper meaning and purpose from within themselves for self-discovery. Amidst the rapid pace of modern life, many people are experiencing a sense of emptiness and disconnection. The evolution of humanity's collective consciousness encourages individuals to look within for re-discovery by rekindling the flame and wonder of self-discovery and aligning their actions with their authentic selves.

Nurturing inner peace and well-being, self-care is a must. The stress and pressures of modern life take a toll on our mental, emotional, physical, and spiritual well-being, causing disease. One's evolution advocates for self-care practices, mindfulness, healing, and meditation or relationship with the divine spirit, empowering individuals to cultivate inner peace and balance. By reconnecting with their inner essence, people can enhance their overall well-being, finding solace in the midst of life's challenges.

Fostering compassion and unity is one of the fundamental tenets of the spiritual revolution, which is the recognition of our interconnectedness. In a world often characterized by division and conflict, embracing this understanding becomes crucial. By transcending societal divisions and embracing compassion, empathy, and understanding, the spiritual evolution of consciousness fosters a sense of unity and harmony among individuals and spiritual communities.

Humanity's collective consciousness as the spiritual warfare crisis looms large calls for a renewed relationship with nature and a shift towards sustainable living. Recognizing that humanity's collective consciousness is intricately intertwined with the natural world, this process emphasizes the importance of ecological awareness, inspiring individuals to adopt eco-friendly practices and become responsible stewards of the Earth.

Challenging materialistic paradigms: this transition challenges the dominant materialistic paradigm that prioritizes external achievements and possessions as markers of success. It encourages individuals to reevaluate their values, focusing on inner growth, personal transformation, and the development of virtues such as gratitude, compassion, kindness, and integrity. By shifting the emphasis from accumulation to inner fulfillment, humanity's evolution seeks to create a more sustainable, balanced, and harmonious society.

In an age where technological advancements continue to reshape our lives, the need for a spiritual evolution becomes increasingly apparent. It provides a path for individuals to rediscover their true essence, fostering inner growth, compassion, and a deeper connection with the world around them. The spiritual revolution holds immense relevance in modern times, offering a guiding light amidst the chaos and providing a framework for personal and societal transformation. By embracing individual evolution through self-discovery, we have the opportunity to create a more harmonious, meaningful, and compassionate world for ourselves and future generations.

This story further revolves around two main characters, Grace and Michael. Grace, a radiant and captivating woman, possesses sandy blonde hair that cascades gracefully around her shoulders. Her mesmerizing eyes reflect a depth of wisdom and compassion that draws people to her. With a shapely body that exudes confidence, she effortlessly embraces her physicality as an expression of self-love and acceptance. Grace possesses a genuine, infectious smile that illuminates any room, effortlessly brightening the spirits of those around her. Having experienced profound loss in her own life, she has emerged stronger, driven by an unwavering desire to guide others toward the path of self-love through self-care and personal awareness. Grace's journey has allowed her to conquer deep-seated pain, and she channels her experiences to inspire and uplift others, becoming a beacon of light, hope, and empowerment.

Michael is a tall, dark, and undeniably handsome man whose outer charm merely hints at the beauty within. Driven by ambition and determination, he has achieved remarkable success in his professional life, possessing everything that most men could ever desire. Yet, despite his accomplishments, Michael finds himself burdened by a profound sense of loneliness and emotional void. Yearning for the intense and meaningful connections he experiences in his fantasies, he embarks on a transformative quest to find the woman of his dreams, quite literally. With a heart that radiates kindness and compassion, Michael seeks not only to fill the void within himself but also to create a love story that transcends the boundaries of his imagination. His journey will take him on an exploration of personal growth, self-discovery, and the realization that true love may be found in unexpected places.

As Grace and Michael's paths intertwine, their individual quests for fulfillment and meaning will converge, setting the stage for a captivating and transformative journey of self-discovery, love, and personal evolution. Together, they will navigate the complexities of their own inner worlds, forging a deep connection that transcends the boundaries of reality and offering each other a chance at healing, profound understanding, and the fulfillment of their deepest desires.

When it comes to Twin Flames connections, there are several powerful signs that signify the unique and profound nature of this relationship. One of the most prominent signs is an intense longing for one's Twin Flame, even when you have already connected with them and sometimes, even when you are physically together. This longing stems from the fact that Twin Flames are two halves of a single human soul, and they yearn for a sense of oneness and unity with each other. This longing is not simply a physical or emotional desire; it is a spiritual and soulful yearning, driving both individuals toward continuous growth and self-improvement.

A key aspect of the Twin Flame connection is the magnetic pull between the souls involved. This pull can be incredibly strong, drawing the two individuals towards each other, even if they have not yet met. It is a deep and mysterious connection that transcends rational understanding. Once Twin Flames come into each other's lives, the attraction and magnetism become undeniable. Even if they separate or go through periods of being apart, the bond remains, and the pull persists. The magnetic connection signifies the inherent need for unity and wholeness that Twin Flames bring to each other's lives.

Another significant sign of a Twin Flame connection is an incredible sense of intuition between the two individuals. It goes beyond mere coincidence; Twin Flames often find themselves thinking or doing the same things simultaneously. They might even have similar dreams or share unspoken understandings. This heightened intuition allows them to have a window into each other's emotional states, sensing when the other is struggling, suffering, or experiencing moments of euphoria. It is a profound connection that transcends ordinary human understanding and deepens the emotional and spiritual bond between Twin Flames.

It's important to note that Twin Flame relationships are not always romantic. In some cases, the connection can manifest as a deep, inseparable friendship. The bond between Twin Flames can be likened to that of siblings, displaying a powerful, intense, and unbreakable connection. This connection is often noticeable to those who observe it, as it carries a unique energy and depth that sets it apart from ordinary friendships.

When Twin Flames meet, they are likely to feel a strong and undeniable recognition of the connection. The bond can be so intense and powerful that both individuals are fully aware of its significance from the very beginning. This awareness, combined with the signs of longing, magnetism, and intuition, reinforces the profound nature of the twin flame relationship. In the journey of Twin Flames, unconditional love, growth, and unity are the guiding forces. It is a transformative and often challenging path, but one that offers the potential for profound personal discovery and spiritual evolution.

The duration of a Twin Flame relationship is not predetermined and can vary greatly from person to person. Unlike soulmate relationships, which are often believed to last a lifetime, Twin Flame connections may or may not endure for an extended period. The purpose of a Twin Flame relationship is often more focused on personal growth and spiritual evolution rather than the longevity of the romantic partnership.

Twin flames often enter each other's lives during times of significant change, conflict, or personal transformation. They may serve as catalysts for personal growth and help individuals transition into new ways of living or being. The intense connection and magnetic attraction experienced in Twin Flame relationships can make trust and intimacy easier to establish compared to other relationships.

However, it's important to note that the path of Twin Flames can be challenging and demanding. The souls that embody Twin Flame connections often have a higher level of spiritual work to undertake. The purpose of this connection is to heal and evolve individually while energetically finding and attracting the other half of their soul. It is a sacred and profound bond that transcends ordinary human connections.

It is worth mentioning that not everyone is fortunate enough to encounter their Twin Flame in their lifetime. Twin Flames are considered rare and magical connections, and not all souls are destined to experience this level of connection and unity. If one is fortunate enough to find their Twin Flame and engage in a romantic relationship, it can be a deeply fulfilling partnership. However, the duration of the relationship will depend on various factors, including the growth and evolution of each individual. Some twin flame relationships may stand the test of time and endure, while others may serve a specific purpose or lesson before potentially transitioning into a different form or coming to a natural conclusion.

Ultimately, the significance and depth of a Twin Flame connection transcend the limitations of human imagination. Experiencing such a connection is considered a profound blessing, bringing forth an extraordinary level of joy, love, and spiritual connection that surpasses ordinary human experiences.

# Chapter 2
# DF and DM Awakening

## *"The Spirit of the Divine Feminine and Masculine Awakening"*

The sun began to rise, casting its golden rays on the world, awakening to a new day and dawning the golden era. The spirit of the Divine Feminine was awakened, ready to rise in all of humanity to bring forth love, cleansing, and healing for every living thing. It was a moment of profound significance, an initiation into a spiritual journey that would forever change her.

For years, she had traversed a path fraught with trials and tribulations, feeling the weight of the world upon her shoulders. Life had tested her in countless ways, pushing her to the brink of despair and challenging her very identity. Through the darkness, a flicker of divine light persisted, guiding her toward this awakening.

It was a process that defied easy description, as it involved a deep and profound transformation of her being. She shed layers of conditioning, societal expectations, and false beliefs that had weighed her down for far too long. Like a phoenix rising from the ashes, she emerged anew, radiating an inner strength and grace that were uniquely her own.

Emotionally, she delved deep into the depths of her soul, unearthing buried wounds and unhealed scars. She faced the demons of her past with unwavering courage, acknowledging the pain and embracing it as a catalyst for growth. Through tears and cathartic release, she reclaimed her emotional sovereignty, granting herself permission to feel deeply and authentically.

Physically, she underwent a metamorphosis. Her body, once tense and rigid, softened and became a vessel of divine feminine energy. She learned to listen to its wisdom, honor its needs, and nurture it with care. Through practices like grounding, martial arts, dance, and embodiment exercises, she tapped into her sensuality, allowing it to flow freely and unapologetically.

The awakening was not merely confined to the physical and emotional realms. It extended to the very core of her being, reaching the depths of her spiritual essence, the very essence of who she was. She connected with her divine intuition, listening intently to the whispers of her soul. Guided by an inner knowing, she danced between realms, exploring the mystical and embracing the mysteries of the universe.

Her journey of self-discovery led her to reclaim the power of her femininity. She embraced the primal force of creation that resided within her, recognizing that she was the source of life, emotion, and intuition. She learned to trust her instincts, honor her cyclical nature, and stand in her authentic truth without apology.

Through this awakening, the Divine Feminine tapped into a wellspring of infinite love, nurturing, and compassion. She realized that these qualities were not weaknesses but strengths, capable of transforming the world around her. As she basked in the radiance of her newfound self, she felt a magnetic pull—a yearning for a connection that went beyond the boundaries of her own existence.

Little did she know that, in the vastness of the universe, the Divine Masculine was also experiencing his awakening. Their paths were destined to converge, their longing for connection and love drawing them inexorably toward one another. For now, she embraced her own transformation, ready to embark on the next chapter of her journey of self-discovery with an open heart and an unwavering belief in the power of her divine feminine essence.

The sun cast its radiant glow upon the Divine Masculine, stirring him from his slumber, feeling an undeniable pull toward something greater. It was as if a dormant force within him had awoken, urging him to embark on a path of self-discovery and purpose.

To connect with his true masculine energy, the Divine Masculine found solace in engaging with the physical world around him. He sought solace in the embrace of nature, where he could witness the grandeur of the universe and reconnect with his primal essence. In the depths of the wilderness, he discovered a sense of grounding and tranquility that eluded him amidst the chaos of everyday life.

With each step he took on the hiking trails and every breath of fresh air he inhaled, the Divine Masculine's energy surged within him. The physical activities he embraced, such as rock climbing, running, and weightlifting, propelled him forward on his journey of awakening. As his muscles strengthened, so too did his connection to his own masculine power.

Through these physical pursuits, the Divine Masculine tapped into his innate desire for achievement and conquest. He set goals for himself, both in his personal and professional life, and dedicated his energy to their attainment. His ambitions became a driving force, propelling him toward success and fulfillment.

As the divine masculine delved deeper into his masculine energy, the Divine Masculine also underwent a profound shift in his mindset and perspective. He realized that true strength did not lie solely in physical powers or dominance but in vulnerability, compassion, and the ability to protect those he loves.

He shed the armor of societal expectations and explored the multifaceted dimensions of his masculine identity. No longer confined by rigid stereotypes, he embraced his emotional depth and cultivated a safe space within himself to express his feelings. This newfound authenticity allowed him to form deeper connections with others, bridging the gap between the masculine and feminine energies within him.

His purpose in life crystallized, no longer driven solely by external accolades or material success. The Divine Masculine understood that his true purpose lay in contributing to the greater good, in being a protector, a provider, and a catalyst for positive change. He recognized that his power was not meant to be wielded in isolation but to be harnessed alongside the Divine Feminine, complementing and balancing each other's energies.

With his masculine energy honed and his purpose embraced, the Divine Masculine stood on the precipice of a transformative journey. His awakening had set him on a collision course with the Divine Feminine, their paths destined to intertwine in a cosmic dance of love and sacred holy divine union. For now, he reveled in the empowerment of his newfound self, ready to embrace the adventure that lay ahead.

As the Divine awakening progressed, the dance of divine union beckoned both of them. Unbeknownst to them, the dreams that filled their nights were not mere figments of their imagination but glimpses of a connection that transcended time and space. In their shared sacred heart, they felt an undeniable longing for each other appearing in their dreams; they are two wholes of the same sacred heart and soul; this holds the key to their soul's deepest desires with a longing for the experience of oneness through their divine unity.

In the depths of their slumber, both the Divine Feminine and the Divine Masculine found themselves immersed in a realm beyond the confines of reality. Night after night, they experienced vivid dreams that transported them to a heavenly place, a sanctuary of ethereal beauty that ignited their souls and evoked a deep sense of belonging.

As the Divine Feminine and the Divine Masculine embarked on their individual journeys of awakening, a profound realization began to dawn upon them. In the depths of their hearts, they recognized that the man and the woman they encountered in their dreams were not mere figments of their imagination but rather an embodiment of the love and magnetic connection they have been pulled towards with a deep longing for one another.

The dreams were a delicate dance, each step bringing them closer to a feeling of oneness that seemed to transcend the boundaries of time and space. Within this celestial realm, they encountered each other, their spirits intertwined in a harmony that resonated with every fiber of their being.

As they danced under the celestial glow, the intensity of their emotions soared. Love, passion, and a profound yearning for a different reality surged through their individual essence. It was a longing that defied rationality, an ache in their hearts that whispered of a connection they couldn't quite comprehend.

Their dreams, so vivid and emotionally charged, felt more real than the waking world around them. The dreams resonated with such authenticity, such raw emotion, that they couldn't dismiss them as mere figments of imagination. Doubt gave way to a growing belief, a flickering hope that whispered of a connection that transcended the boundaries of their current reality. It was in the dancing dreams, in the connection they felt with each other, that they finally glimpsed the flames of passion and love that had eluded them for so long.

With each passing day, the veil between dreams and waking life grew thinner. The world they once knew began to blur as their hearts yearned for a truth that eluded them. The dreams had become an integral part of their existence, a guiding light in the darkness, pulling them toward a destiny that awaited their embrace.

Within the depths of their awakened souls, the Divine Feminine and the Divine Masculine carried the weight of past traumas that had shaped the very fabric of their beings. These experiences had left indelible marks upon their hearts, etching scars that whispered of pain and loss, and ready to embark on their individual healing journey.

They began to understand that their dreams were not mere fantasies but glimpses into a divine reality, a destiny that awaited them. The universe conspires to bring them together, to awaken their souls, and to guide them toward a profound holy union. Yet, even as the Divine Feminine and the Divine Masculine reveled in this newfound knowledge, a sense of trepidation tinged their excitement. They knew that the path ahead would not be without its challenges. The forces that sought to keep them apart would test their resolve, throwing obstacles in their way. They would be forced to confront their own fears, insecurities, and the wounds of their past.

Armed with a knowing of a sacred divine union, the twins stood ready to face whatever lay ahead. They were willing to traverse the stormy seas and scale the highest mountains in pursuit of a love that defied all odds through their own self-love. The dance of their dreams had awakened a yearning within them, a longing for a reality where their souls intertwined in perfect harmony, dancing through eternity as One.

# Chapter 3
# The Search Within

The air crackled with anticipation as the twins embarked on their quest for each other through their own self-discovery. Their hearts yearned for a connection that went beyond the confines of their dreams, a sacred love that beckoned them forward with an irresistible pull. Guided by an invisible force, they set out on a journey of discovery, determined to find one another and unite their souls.

In moments of quiet solitude, they could feel the other's presence, with a thread of destiny woven them together, binding their souls across time and space. It was a magnetic force that transcended rationality, a deep knowing that their paths were destined to converge. With each passing day of their individual healing, their intuition sharpened, guiding them toward signs and synchronicities that confirmed they were on the right track. They noticed repeated numbers, serendipitous encounters, and vivid dreams that further fueled their quest toward divine union through self-healing. This paved the way, leading them closer to the elusive connection they sought first within themselves.

Yet, the path was not without its challenges. Obstacles stood as tests along their journey, threatening to block their sacred union that is a GOD-given gift. External circumstances played their part, placing geographical distance or societal expectations in their way. It was the internal battles that proved most formidable—their own fears, insecurities, and past wounds that whispered doubts into their hearts.

In the face of these obstacles, the twins exhibited resilience and determination. They refused to let fear overshadow their desire for love and connection. With an unwavering belief in the power of their bond, they pressed forward, step by step, even when the path seemed treacherous and uncertain.

The twins' individual growth became their strength. As they confronted their internal struggles, they shed old patterns and limiting beliefs that held them back. Through self-reflection and healing, they gained clarity and a deeper understanding of themselves. Their journey of self-discovery intertwined with each step forward, revealing more of their authentic selves.

The greatest challenges they encountered were the ones within themselves. Fear, doubt, and past wounds gnawed at their resolve, casting shadows on their path. In moments of vulnerability, they questioned whether they were deserving of such a profound sacred love. They grappled with the fear of rejection, of being seen fully and authentically.

When doubts threatened to consume them, they found solace in confiding in trusted friends who understood their quest. These confidantes offered encouragement, lending a listening ear and reminding them of the strength within their hearts. As they overcame the obstacles one by one, their determination burned brighter. So, they pressed on, their hearts ablaze with the promise of love in a divine union that held the potential to transform their lives.

As their quest continued, their longing intensified, fueling their drive to find each other. With every sunrise and every starlit night, their desire grew, their souls intertwining even more deeply within their dreams, dancing in the heavenly realm. They could sense that they were drawing closer, that their connection was on the verge of being realized.

Yet, it was precisely in moments of darkness that their strength shone through. They summoned courage from the depths of their beings, confronting their insecurities head-on. They embarked on a journey of self-discovery, delving into the wounds that held them back, determined to heal and grow.

Through introspection and self-reflection, they realized that their connection went beyond the physical realm. It was a soul-deep bond, a spiritual union that beckoned them toward each other. In their dreams, they caught glimpses of this ethereal connection, their spirits entwined in a dance of longing and love.

With every obstacle they overcame, the Twins' grew internally stronger and more determined. The flame of their desire burned brighter, propelling them forward on their journey. They had come too far to turn back now. In the midst of their individual growth and the battles they faced, the Twins could sense their union drawing closer.

The energy crackled in the air, a magnetic force urging them onward. They knew that the meeting they yearned for was on the horizon, their souls aligning with the rhythm of the universe.
So, with hearts ablaze and spirits resilient, they pressed on. The twins' journey was not without its share of obstacles and challenges, testing their resolve and commitment to themselves to heal what no longer served their highest good.

External circumstances seemed determined to keep them apart, weaving a tapestry of complexities that demanded their unwavering determination. Geographical distance stood as a formidable barrier, stretching between them like an ocean they had to traverse. The twins found themselves in different corners of the world, longing for the touch and presence of the other. Yet, their souls remained intertwined, bridging the physical gap with the invisible thread of connection.

Societal expectations and cultural norms also cast shadows on their path. They were warned of the risks of defying conventions, of pursuing a love that challenged established boundaries. The twins refused to succumb to the limitations imposed upon them. They dared to follow the yearnings of their hearts, to honor the pull of destiny that drew oneness from within themselves closer with each passing day.

Yet, the greatest obstacles they faced were the internal struggles that threatened to undermine their pursuit of love. Past wounds and traumas resurfaced, testing their emotional resilience. Fear, insecurities, and the scars of previous heartbreaks whispered doubts into their hearts, tempting them to retreat to familiar yet unfulfilling shores.

It was in these moments of darkness that the Twins' strength and determination truly shone. They confronted their inner demons head-on, refusing to let them dictate their destiny. Each obstacle they encountered became an opportunity for growth and self-discovery as they embraced their vulnerabilities and learned to heal their wounded hearts.

With every obstacle conquered, their spirits soared higher. The Twins could feel the universe conspiring in their favor, the energy shifting in their favor. The forces that once stood as barriers now seemed to align, guiding them closer to their long-awaited union. As the Twins overcame the obstacles in their path, their determination and resilience propelled them forward, inching them ever closer to the realization of their profound holy reunion. The time had come to bridge the final divide and embrace the unconditional love they had sought for so long.

As the Twins overcame these obstacles in their path, their determination and resilience propelled them forward, inching them ever closer to the realization of their profound union. The time had come to bridge the final divide and embrace the love they had sought for so long.

They had weathered the storms of doubt, traversed the winding roads of uncertainty, and emerged stronger on the other side. The challenges they faced tested their commitment and strengthened them by trusting their inner knowledge and guidance. The Twins had grown individually, shedding layers of insecurity and fear as they embraced the depth of their own newfound worthiness with purpose.

The challenges they had overcome served as stepping stones to their reunion. They understood that the obstacles were not meant to keep them apart but to deepen their appreciation for the love they had longed for.

With their heavenly encounters and spiritual connection paving the way, the twins stood on the threshold of a transformative holy reunion. The anticipation in the air was palpable, as if the universe held its breath, waiting for their souls to intertwine in an exquisite dance of love and connection in all dimensions and aspects of self.

# Chapter 4
# Twin Flames Reunion

Twin Flames reunions have begun after millions of years apart. They're having dreams, and they're finding themselves reuniting for a grand purpose to assist humanity into the golden era, the age of Aquarius, into a new world with a new way of being. Twin Flames has the purpose of assisting humanity back to its true nature of unconditional love. Twin Flames share one sacred heart and human soul; their core vibration is exactly the same. They have been separated by the source of all that is, GOD, to experience and observe itself through different aspects of the soul's growth and evolution. This love is the new order of things from now on as humanity moves forward into the golden ages.

The purpose of Twin Flames' divine reunion is to exemplify unconditional love and raise the collective consciousness of humanity by being the way-showers and creating heaven on earth. This occurrence happens through unconditional love through their sacred heart and holy divine reunion. A new reality is being born, and it's rebirthing through Christ's consciousness.

Christ's consciousness encompasses qualities such as unconditional love, compassion, forgiveness, and an awareness of the interconnectedness of all beings. It is a higher level of awareness and consciousness that transcends ego and separation, leading to a deeper understanding of the divine truths and the unity of all of creation.

Embodying Christ's consciousness is attained through the Nine Fruits of the Holy Spirit, which are love, joy, peace, forbearance, kindness, goodness, faithfulness, gentleness, and, my personal favorite, self-control.

The Twins' individual journeys are fraught with challenges, with divine guidance always clears a path through their hardships. Making them pillars of light on their own. Having divine guidance will lead them to their long-awaited soul reunion. Twin Flames sacred reunions, the second coming of Christ consciousness, have been prophesied by our ancestors for eons anticipated by existence itself. We will see this in the continuing love story of the twins, Grace and Michael.

The air was charged with a new and fresh clearing energy of transformation. The Twins individually feel the excitement from the overjoyed emotions they were feeling for their best friend's and confidant's upcoming wedding. The Twins were unknowingly getting ready for the same wedding. The wedding of Grace's best friend and confidant, Emma, and Michael's best friend, Caleb. They have been best friends since childhood, and yet Grace and Michael have never met through Emma and Caleb. The Twins had no idea what was about to occur in this divinely inspired encounter that awaited them on this magical evening. An evening that would shift and change their lives forever.

The Twins arrived at Emma and Caleb's wedding, which would be starting shortly, giving the Twins the opportunity to wish their best friends a happy life full of love. Grace opened the door to the bridal suite, seeing Emma standing there in her beautiful wedding gown, including a jeweled crown her grandmother had given her to wear; it was the same one she wore at her own wedding. Of course, Grace could not hold back the tears of joy with Emma standing there looking so angelic with the expression of excitement and love on her glowing face.

"You are the most beautiful bride I've ever seen. You look gorgeous, like an elegant queen! I'm so happy for you and Caleb. I pray GOD will send the one I am destined to be with." Grace shared.

"You mean the Man in your dreams, the one you have been dancing with beyond the gates of heaven?" Emma asked Grace. She nodded, agreeing with Emma.

"You never know who and when GOD will send your dream person into your life. Grace, you know it's about divine timing. I do know one thing for certain: that you're destined for a great love. That love Is out there dreaming, praying, and searching for you and connecting to your heart's desires. I just know it, Grace." Emma said, ensuring Grace.

Emma hugged Grace, telling her, "I love you, Grace." Grace responded with, "I love you too, Emma. Are you ready to walk down the aisle to your true love?" Emma responded with, "I AM."

The wedding ceremony took place in a sacred cathedral and included the wedding couple being adorned in traditional wedding attire. The groom wears a black tuxedo with a white shirt and black bow tie. The bride wore a flowing, elegant ivory lace gown, complete with her crown and long veil; Emma was accompanied down the aisle by the adorable flower girl.

The sacred cathedral was adorned with soft ivory decorations and featured elaborate floral arrangements and tall candelabras.

Soft, sacred music fills the air as the bride and groom exchange vows in front of a large, holy, symbolic stained-glass window.

Friends and family were beaming with joy to witness this union between Emma and Caleb, their faces glowing with love and joy beneath the soft candlelight. The Twins took their seats to witness this sacred event, and they kept brushing alongside each other without noticing each other. Grace couldn't stop the flow of happy tears through the whole wedding ceremony. Michael's eyes were getting misty, and he wasn't just witnessing this wedding; he couldn't stop daydreaming of dancing with the woman in his dreams. Wondering if this love and person will ever materialize in his life.

The wedding ceremony ended, and it was beautiful, holy, and sacred. It was now time to head to the reception to celebrate with the bride and groom on their divine union. The evening wedding reception is held in a beautifully adorned ballroom with white lights twinkling overhead, creating a warm and inviting atmosphere. The room is filled with a soft glow of candles, placed elegantly on each table, adding to the magical ambiance of the celebratory event.

Grace and Michael enter the ballroom, brushing up beside each other with a near miss once again, both unaware that standing right next to them was their heart's desire and the lover of their soul. As they walked into the reception, it immediately transported the Twins into a dreamy dance state of heavenly romance and beauty, creating an intense energy rising in both of them.

The sound of angelic harps, cellos, and pianos floats through the air as the musicians skillfully play together, creating a beautiful and harmonious melody that sets the tone for this magical evening. The newlyweds take to the dance floor for their first dance as a married couple. Everyone watches in awe, moved by the beauty and romance, while witnessing the newly destined union of Emma and Caleb. This immediately took Grace and Michael to their dream state in the Heavenly realm, dancing with the person they are certain is as real as each breath they take.

White lights twinkle overhead, casting a warm glow over the room, while scented candles fill the air with a sweet fragrance of jasmine and lavender. The evening continued with more music and dancing, with the sounds of laughter and the buzz of happiness, and all of a sudden, the people on the dance floor started to part, creating a clearing for across the room, and it happened: Michael and Grace finally locked eyes.

First, they are overwhelmed with rushing energies through their whole being. Wide-eyed with wonder, they slowly rose from their chairs; as they approached one another, their hearts raced in unison as an intense, unseen, magnetic force urged them forward together. With every step, an overwhelming sense of familiarity washed over them, feeling a melody they had known since the beginning of time. The feelings rising in them was an extremely intense sexual energy; it was warm and overwhelming as they gazed into each other's eyes from opposite ends of the dance floor. It was a recognition that transcended the physical realm and dimension, an inexplicable connection that defied rational explanation.

Their hands reached out instinctively, drawn together by a divine force. As their fingers intertwined, a surge of energy passed between them, confirming the depth of their connection. A divine melody song was playing, and it was like they'd danced to this song together forever, and they danced without saying a word. It was so intense it created energetic orgasms in each one of their chakras, energy centers, almost making them feel faint and weak in the knees, while both of them experienced goosebumps from their energy's convergence, creating quite the erotic electrical current.

They didn't have to speak; their nonverbal communication was loud and clear. It was intensely romantic, erotic, sublime, and sacred. Their souls dance in harmony as if performing a long-awaited dance duet. They were the divine symphony that echoed through the ages, and their reunion was the crescendo that would forever mark their existence.

Time was non-existent, and the world faded into the background as they took in each other's features. At that moment, the energetic puzzle pieces of their true essence were reconnecting and revealing the long-awaited love they had knowingly yearned for. Tears welled up in their eyes as emotions surged within both of their heart chakra. Joy, relief, and a profound sense of belonging intertwined in a whirlwind of captivating feelings. It was as if they were not meeting for the first time but rather reuniting after eons of separation.

Their embrace transcended the physical as if their soul recognized each other long before their conscious mind and bodies did. In the tender silence that enveloped them, they felt the weight of their shared past, the years they had spent unknowingly apart. Yet, in the face of their divine reunion, those years seemed inconsequential, dwarfed by the magnitude of the present moment.

As they gazed into each other's eyes, they saw reflections of themselves—a mirrored image that held the key to their identity. They were no longer alone in the world; they were home; they were a part of a greater cosmic whole, connected by an unbreakable bond of unconditional love that had been bestowed upon their shared Soul by GOD itself.

Grace reached out to touch Michael's cheek, her fingers tracing the lines of his face as if to confirm his existence. "You're real," she whispered, her voice filled with wonder. He smiled, a mix of emotions dancing in his eyes, not able to hold back tears of joy. "And so are you," he replied, his thumb gently brushing away the tears of joy that escaped her eyes as well. "We're real, and we're finally together," Michael said. "I have dreamt about us and waited forever and a day for this sacred, holy reunion moment with you."

In this moment of revelation, they knew that their lives would never be the same. The depth of their connection was undeniable, and they were both acutely aware of the impact it would have on their future and the future of humanity.

Their dreams had served as an awakening bridge, transcending time and distance to bring them together in the most extraordinary way. It was a connection that seemed to defy the boundaries of reality, and they marveled at the beauty of the universe's intricate design between the divine feminine and divine masculine reunion.

"It's like we've been living two lives, connected through these dreams," Grace marveled, her eyes searching for understanding in her newfound intimacy with the other part of her soul.

Michael nodded, his heart swelling with a sense of wonder and excitement. "I've felt your presence in my dreams as we danced within heaven's gate, and now that I see you before me, it all makes sense. We were destined to find each other."

"I've missed you so much," Grace confessed with tears in her eyes, her voice choking with emotion. "Even though I didn't know you existed, I felt your absence and presence deep within my heart and soul."

Michaels's eyes softened with tenderness as he gently wiped away her tears. "And I've missed you too, more than you'll ever know," he whispered. "Even when I didn't know who you were, I felt a void that only you could fill in my life, the one I want to dance through eternity with. I've felt you with every part of my being."

Michael leaned in, giving Grace a passionate kiss; nothing else existed except this grand love of their divine reunion created by unconditional love.

As the emotional currents flowed between them, they discovered an unshakable love that seemed to grow with every passing moment. It was a love that transcended time and space, a love that had been woven into the fabric of their beings by GOD long before they had the chance to recognize it.

Their reunion was a cosmic miracle, a supernatural divine reunion of their souls' sacred hearts that had once been divided for the purpose of evolution, and they are now reunited in this holy presence of love.

As the evening unwinded, Grace and Michael both approached the newlyweds, Emma and Caleb. Emma excitedly said, "You finally met each other. Wow, you both looked great on the dance floor. Like you've danced before. "Emma said with a giggle and a wink at Grace. Grace leaned into Emma's ear, whispering, "He's the man in my dreams!"

Michael expressed how beautiful the wedding was and congratulated the Newlyweds. Grace asked Emma, "When will you be leaving for your honeymoon?" Emma responded, "We are leaving now." with a big smile on Emma's face, she said to Grace, "When we get back from our trip, I want to hear every lovely detail about this beautiful miracle; my heart smiles for you." Grace nodded yes. Michael hugged Caleb, congratulating him again on his divine union with Emma. Wishing the newlyweds a safe and beautiful honeymoon.

As the newlyweds said their goodbyes, exiting the celebratory event. Grace looked up at Michael and asked, "Now, what do we do?" Michael replied, "Whatever we want." he said with a handsome smirk. Grace extended an invitation, "My home is just a couple blocks away if you'd like to walk me home." she said blushingly. "We can share and get to know more about ourselves at my place because I don't want you to be out of reach anymore. I just found you, and I don't want this night to end. I want to be by your side always," she told him. Michael smiled and responded, "I can't think of anything better than to be in your presence, my love. I don't want to leave your side either." Michael took her by the hand, and they proceeded with a wonderful full moonlit night walk to Grace's house.

As the jubilant melodies from the wedding reception faded behind them, Grace and Michael stepped out into the summer night hand in hand. Their eyes twinkled with affectionate glances, still enveloped in the magic of their dear friends' union. Radiating with joy, they meandered through the idyllic garden, their footsteps accompanied by the gentle rustle of leaves and distant laughter. Each gentle breeze adds an ethereal touch to their stroll. Amidst the lush surroundings, the couple's conversation wove through anecdotes and dreams for their own future. Hand in hand, they continued their leisurely journey back to Grace's, cherishing this intimate moment of togetherness through their sacred unity and looking forward to their own adventure as partners for all of eternity.

As they made their way inside Grace's home, they got themselves comfortable starting a cozy fire and putting on some lovely relaxing music; Grace offered Michael a glass of wine. She lit some candles and slipped into something more comfortable. When she returned to the living room, Michael stood up, stunned by her beauty, "You are so beautiful," Grace blushed, then asked, "Grace, would you honor me with another dance?" Putting down his glass of wine, he was already intoxicated by Grace's presence, as was she in his, feeling secure in his arms. Grace responded with, "Yes, Michael, I will dance through eternity with you." They held each other in a warm embrace, swaying slowly in the contentment of the blissful presence of each other's embrace. This was just the beginning of something prophetic and profound for both their souls' evolution and self-discovery journeys.

As Twin Flames come together, they feel a deep and profound connection, like magnets being irresistibly drawn to one another. The energy between them crackles with electrical intensity, and a sense of divine passion expresses itself. They have reached a stage where their souls are ready to merge on a higher level.

The Twins were filled with intense passion, and they stayed up all night, holding each other, slow dancing, and exchanging stories of tribulations and victories.

They both shared that they've written love letters to each other to express their longing for such a connection of divine unity and oneness in their love letters to each other.

A love letter from Grace to Michael:

"Lover of my soul, the man of my dreams, I sit here, unknown to your face, unaware of your name; I find solace in knowing that you are out there somewhere, waiting for our paths to finally intertwine. It is with an eager heart that I write this love letter to the man who holds the key to my sacred heart, a love I know exists yet have not had the pleasure of meeting. My one and only who dances with me in my dreams. I can feel you, my love.

I long to hold your hand, to feel the warmth of your touch. To get lost in your eyes and see the reflection of a love so pure that it takes our breath away. In my dreams, I envision the way your laughter will fill the room, bringing joy to every corner of our existence. Your voice, like a soothing melody, will resonate within my sacred heart, reminding me that we were destined to find one another for a greater purpose.

I yearn for the moments we will share, both big and small memories that we create with our love. The quiet evenings spent by the fireplace, wrapped in each other's arms, hearts beating in unison as one.

Though I may not know your face or the sound of your laughter just yet, I am filled with unwavering hope that our paths will cross in the most serendipitous of ways. Until that fateful moment, I will keep the flame of love alive within me, knowing that you, my one true love, are out there, searching for me just as ardently.

I trust in the magic of the universe, confident that our love story will be extraordinary, far beyond anything we could ever have imagined. I love you so much." Grace read the letter, and Michael, feeling so moved in his heart, held Grace closer.

Grace said to Michael, "We're a cosmic force bound together by the all. Our love has the power to inspire, uplift, and transform not only our lives but also those around us."

Michael responded, "Let us embrace this rare and extraordinary gift we have been given, cherishing every moment of our shared journey. Together, we shall traverse the ebbs and flows of life, embracing the challenges and celebrating the victories; I desire love with no bounds or limitations."

"Grace, I would like to read a love letter I wrote to you. You are my dream come true, and I feel so honored and privileged to have finally found you to experience a love that knows no bounds."

A love letter from Michael to Grace:

Michael read his love letter to Grace aloud, "It isn't easy being so in love with you and not being able to see you every day. There are times when I'd give anything just to be able to gaze into your eyes or hold you in my arms, even for a few minutes. I always feel incomplete, like a part of me is missing when we're not together. I know that right now, this is how things have to be, but that doesn't make it any easier to bear. Every day without you reminds me of the joy that I'm missing. So don't forget that I love you, that I'm thinking of you, and that I'm counting every minute until we're together again." Their soul was home and complete with the love it desired and longed for, bringing alignment in the cosmos with all that is in this very moment.

As the sun rises, the Twins have work obligations. Michael explained, "Grace, my love, I have to go to the office. I have deadlines and meetings. I don't want to leave you. Let me make it up to you and send a car for you this evening. I will plan a Magical evening together. I have something very special I want to put together for our official first reuniting date."

Michael asks, "So, my love, what say you? Are you willing to step into this realm of enchantment with me? If your heart sings with a resounding 'yes,' then join me in making memories that will linger in our soul forever." Grace said not a word and kissed him passionately with an obvious "Yes, I accept." Neither one could stop kissing the other from this strong magnetic pull to each other, and it would be a date that they'd never forget.

# Chapter 5
# The Enchanted Evening

As Twin Flames reunite and embark on their Sacred comic dance. Our Twins, Grace and Michael, are eagerly preparing for their official first date; an electric charge of anticipation fills their bodies with erotic excitement and an unprecedented sense of wonder. Michael finds his mind consumed with thoughts of Grace, unable to focus on anything else due to the swirling mix of euphoric arousal and intense desire that engulfs him. Fortunately, his faithful secretary assists him with the arrangements for the evening. Meanwhile, Grace, fully immersed in a state of bliss, decides to call off work, knowing that she cannot concentrate on anything other than Michael and the overwhelming anticipation of their enchanted evening to experience this magically sacred reunion orchestrated by the cosmic engineer.

As Grace prepared for her highly anticipated first date with Michael, the man she knew to be the embodiment of her deepest desires, an intoxicating mix of nerves and delicious excitement coursed through her veins. Every fiber of her being ached with a primal longing to experience the sheer intensity of their connection, a connection that had been tantalizingly nurtured through their passionate conversations and seductive dances within the realms of their shared, altered state of reality behind heaven's gate.

This night deserves a fabulously over-the-top dress. "What's a girl to wear?" Grace purrs playfully to her four-legged sidekick.

In front of her closet, Grace stands, surrounded by a tantalizing feast of possibilities. Her fingers caress the silky fabrics and delicate lace that drape her collection of dresses; each imbued with memories of passionate encounters from nights past.

And then, as if by divine intervention, her gaze falls upon a dress concealed in the deepest recesses of her wardrobe. Its scarlet hue, ready to blaze as sensual radiate fire, beaming aura of untamed desire. It beckons to her, whispering promises of passion and a seductive allure that would captivate Michael's heart in an instant. Grace, always one to wear her emotions on her sleeve, knows that this dress carries an enchantment of its own—a supernatural charisma that exudes confidence and unabashed sensuality.

Grace knew that the key to creating the perfect aura of irresistibility for her enchanted evening with Michael was to enlist the services of the enigmatic magician of fashion, Toni. With every skillful stroke of his brush, Toni superbly transformed Grace's hair into a mesmerizing cascade of elegant, seductive waves, perfectly complementing the sparkle in her eyes and sultry red dress. As Grace caught a glimpse of herself in the mirror, she knew with perfect certainty that, under Toni's expert touch, she was more than just ready to ignite the undeniable passions that awaited her and Michael.

Toni said, "Oh, Grace, I think you are my best creation yet. You look ravishing, darling. I can only imagine how breathtaking you will be in that fiery red dress. Now, we're sure every moment of your time with Michael will be filled with irresistible enchantment."

"Is there anything else I can assist you with, lovely lady?" Grace looked in the mirror and felt transported in her state of mind; she saw a glimpse of something new and familiar. Grace had a feeling of passionate sacredness beaming through her beauty and innocence to the love she was destined to experience with Michael. She felt electrified with wonder at this new season of her life and what was to unfold in ways that were unimaginable.

The car arrived to take Grace to her enchanted date destination. She heard the knock at the door, and when she opened the door, there he was, the man of her dreams, literally, with a beautiful bouquet of flowers and a very charming smile. His eyes dazzled in delight to see the beauty and love that stood before him. The surges of erotic pleasure were almost too much to contain for Michael. Little did he know Grace was feeling electrifyingly aroused like never before; it's an undeniable connection, a purely sacred and holy spiritual connection.

They are not acting impulsively on their erotic arousal because the foundation of a Twin Flame love relationship and convergence is honoring this love, giving it time to unfold and bloom. Practicing one of the fruits of the holy spirit, self-control. This love is an unfolding of their shared sacred heart and should be honored.

Michael, looking at Grace, says, "Wow! I don't have any words, Grace, you are so elegantly angelic!" with an excited and amazingly pleased look on his face, and he leaned in for a passionate I missed your kiss. Grace, blushing, says, "Thank you, you look so handsome." Touching his face to ensure he was really here, giving him another passionate kiss. Once their lips parted, Grace said, "I feel I am in a heavenly dream, my love." "Are your dreams coming true, Grace?" He said with a cute smirk. Grace replied, "Right before my eyes." Michael put his arm out for

Grace to escort her to the car, opening the door for her, and now on to their way to their special destination

They are transcended to where time stands still, their dream fantasies coming true to life; this is where magic intertwines with true reality, so to speak. In this realm of enchantment, it will be a wondrous journey for the Twins. They would be under the mysterious glow of a thousand twinkling stars, dancing beneath the ethereal moonlight, embarking on an adventure filled with beauty, wonder, and the intoxicating fragrance of pure romantic and blissful joy.

Their destination was in a hidden garden, concealed from the outside world, where nature's secrets whisper delightfully in their ears. It was a warm summer evening, and the air was filled with the melodious chirping of birds and the sweet fragrance of nearby flowers.

As they stroll hand-in-hand, they are serenaded by the gentle melodies of nature itself, harmonizing with the beats of their unified hearts. The air brimmed with laughter, joy, and a sense of childlike wonder, with unimaginable excitement. In the air, there was a gentle breeze of the sweet fragrance of blooming flowers, and the gentle breeze whispered promises of something extraordinary to come. As they enter the grand garden, a vision of ethereal beauty unfolds before their eyes.

The garden was like a scene from their dancing dreams behind heaven's gate, with pathways adorned with delicate rose petals in various hues, leading them through shimmering fountains that create a soothing symphony. The garden was filled with the glow of candles elegantly shimmering for a magical ambiance of this holy, sacred evening.

In the center of the garden, under a gracefully draped gazebo, a table for two is impeccably set with fine china, crystal glasses, and elegant silverware. A cascading floral centerpiece made up of white roses, fragrant jasmine, and vibrant orchids acts as a stunning focal point.

Just as they were to take their seats, a gentle angelic harp melody began to play, emanating a beautiful love song melody that sounded divine. Michael stopped and asked, "Grace, would you honor me with a dance here on our own private dance floor?" "I would be delighted, Michael," Grace answered.

Grace looked up at Michael and said., "You have created such a romantic and heartwarming evening for us. Thank you, Michael." Giving him a sweet and sincere hug of gratitude. "You've made me feel very special, Michael," he replied. "Our magical night is just beginning, my love; we're just getting started, darling."

The Twins find themselves in a constant state of pure bliss. Taking their seats across from each other, their eyes locked in a dance of affection and anticipation. As they savor each bite of their delectable meal, shared laughter fills the air. The sound of their mirth intertwines with soft background music, creating a symphony of joy and unbreakable connection.

With every shared joke and amusing story, their smiles grow wider, the corners of their lips crinkling with the sheer delight of their shared happiness. Their eyes sparkle with a warmth that radiates from the depths of their soul, a silent language of adoration and affection.

Between bites, their hands reach out, brushing against each other's hands, a subtle yet constant form of contact that speaks volumes of their desire to be connected. Their gestures are gentle, each touch infused with a tenderness that elicits shivers of pleasure up and down their energy centers; it's quite an energetic orgasmic experience.

Time faded into insignificance as they revel in the beauty of their togetherness. Their connection transcends the mundane and enters a realm of its own, a precious sanctuary of love and understanding.

As the evening progresses, Michaels's heart beats with a mixture of excitement and nervous anticipation. His gaze lingers upon the woman he adores, taking in every delicate detail of her beauty. With each passing moment, he feels the depth of his love for her growing, and he yearns to take their relationship to new heights without hesitation; she's the One, and he's the One.

In this enchanted evening of magical romance and powerful, intense love, anticipation heightens every sensation, leaving the Twins trembling with excitement and longing. The stage is set, the stars aligned, and as the night unfolds, you know that this will be a night to remember – a night where dreams intertwine with reality and love weaves its own enchanting experience.

Grace and Michael are surrounded by an ambiance of love's magic and enchantment; the Twins embrace the intoxicating atmosphere of their romantic evening. The soft glow of candlelight flickers, casting warm hues upon their faces as they share stories, laughter, and sweet glances.

As the evening unfolds, their eyes lock in moments of shared intimacy and a profound sense of knowing. Each look is a testament to the depth of their bond, a silent vow to cherish and treasure the love they have found. They are not merely savouring delicious food; they are nourishing their souls. They are relishing the simple yet profound joy of being in each other's company, where the world around them fades away, and their love takes center stage.

Summoning his courage, he reaches out to hold her hand, his touch tender yet determined. At that moment, their connection deepens as a jolt of energy consumes their being and becomes entirely intertwined, dancing to the same shared rhythm of their sacred heart vibes.

Still holding her hand, he gathered the courage and said, "Grace, I know we just met face to face yesterday, and this being our first date and all, it is by far the best day ever, and you know I love you from the depth of my heart, and I know you love me so much, our love is undeniable. So, I don't want another moment to go by being apart from each other; my heart's desire is to embark on our spiritual, sacred journey together every step of the way. What I'm trying to say is I want you; it's always been you, and I want all of you. You've made me feel like a Twitter-pated teenager with constant goose bumps, feeling weak in the knees, and I can't think straight; you make me feel such arousal and excitement. I didn't even know some of these feelings existed. I want to make sweet, passionate love with you. I want us to do it the way that honours our sacred reunion."

Grace was smiling with tears of joy streaming down her cheeks and the feeling of powerful violet flame arousal in her heart; her love for him sparkled in her eyes like a sky full of shining diamonds.

As their eyes lock deeper, his voice takes on a vulnerable tone, revealing the depth of his emotions. "I want to ask you something," his voice shook from intense excitement and anticipation. "There is a place, a haven of tranquillity and beauty, where I wish for us to escape to. I want you all to myself, and I want to give you all your heart desires and more." He gave her an irresistible, charming smile.

"A destination where time slows, allowing us to be fully present in each other's arms, which would be a dream come true for both of us. A place where our love can bloom and flourish with ecstasy as we explore the depths of our desires and make passionate love. I have dreamed of passionately kissing you and loving you for so long; finally, the divine time to love you is finally here." Michael explained with a strong heart's desire.

"I've prepared a private, secluded place that is all tranquil and just for us. We can stay the whole weekend if you'd like. Please say 'Yes,' and make me the happiest I've ever been in my life. We can go by your place and pick up your things, of course, and you can pack what you'll need." He smiles nervously. "Don't leave me in suspense, say 'Yes' Grace, say you will come away with me.

Let's dance together under the mysterious glow under a blanket of shining stars; let us dance beneath the ethereal moonlight. We shall embark on an adventure filled with beauty, wonder, and the intoxicating fragrance of divine love."

Grace, of course, was all for a weekend of endless sensual lovemaking. However, she was speechless; she answered by nodding yes to his invitation, confirming and RSVP'ing with a kiss.

In these moments, they are reminded of the magic that lies within their divine reunion, grateful for the laughter and smiles that seem to flow endlessly, painting their shared journey with strokes of happiness and contentment.

Their enchanting evening is winding down, Grace catching her heart's breath to say, "This was such a beautifully romantic date; you made me feel loved and special. Thank you, Michael." Leaning in for a sweet kiss of gratitude. "I don't want this feeling to end. I choose you, Michael; you've treated me like a queen since we walked out onto the dance floor at Emma and Caleb's wedding reception. You make me feel feelings I didn't know I had within me, too. It's always been you, too, winking and smiling at him. "With every dance we've danced behind heaven's gate within our dreams, I fell more in love with you, every sacred dance we shared." Her eyes widened with excited anticipation, blushing appearing across her cheeks again as his intentions weaved their way into her heart.

The words hung in the air, pregnant with emotion and the promise of a future filled with unconditional love, loyalty, compassion, and contentment. Time seems to stand still as they both share a moment of silent anticipation, a symphony of both their hearts beating in unison, arousing feelings of infinite ecstasy.

Michael kissed Grace on the hand, telling her, "You feel like home." kissing her hand again, "Are you ready to start this adventurous journey of divine love together?" Grace took her hand and stroked the side of his face, saying, "I was born ready to love you, Michael, and my love, you shall have."

Hand in hand, they walked out onto the dance floor, ending this enchanting evening, taking with them a whirlwind of romance and passion. They were now getting ready to experience an explosion of the best love in existence, created from an unbreakable bond from GOD'S own unconditional love.

# Chapter 6
# Kundalini Awakening

The age of Aquarius, where the light prevails over darkness with liberation for humanity and the planet from enslavement and suffering. This is the Twins' purpose: to be way-showers by creating heaven on earth by exemplifying Christ's consciousness.

Twins have the Kundalini Awakening, which is a mystical experience that involves the rising of a powerful dormant spiritual energy residing at the base of the spine, often represented as a coiled serpent. You see this symbol everywhere in reference to medical care. When Kundalini is awakened and activated, this potent energy ascends through the chakra system, energizing and awakening various aspects of the self. Kundalini can be seen as a transformative force, leading to spiritual growth, higher consciousness, and even mystical experiences.

While Kundalini energy can include and activate sexual energy within it, it's important to understand that sexual energy extends beyond the scope of Kundalini alone. Sexual energy can be expressed and experienced in various ways, not solely limited to Kundalini awakening.

Kundalini and sexual energy—are two powerful forces that can intertwine and yet also have their own unique and distinct characteristics.

On the other hand, sexual energy refers specifically to the vitality and life force energy associated with our sexual desires, attractions, and experiences. It encompasses our physical, emotional, and energetic aspects and has the potential to bring immense pleasure, connection, and creativity into our lives.

Both Kundalini and sexual energy are powerful forces that, when consciously channelled and balanced, can lead to personal growth, spiritual evolution, and intensified intimacy. It's a beautifully intricate dance.

With Twin Flames, Kundalini energy activation can be seen as a catalyst for spiritual growth and a deepening of the connection between the Twin Flames. When both individuals are together, Kundalini can create a powerful, magical, energetic bond and further align their energies, emotions, and consciousness with the source of all that is.

For Twin Flames, the Kundalini awakening can be a powerful and transformative experience, as it can lead to greater awareness, spiritual growth, and reunion of the Twins. When both Twins experience a Kundalini activation, they may feel a deep sense of unity and connection with each other, even when physically apart, as their energies merge and become the sacred convergence of their soul. This convergence is the most powerful energy in existence. This is not just a physical and emotional experience; it's universally powerful and Spiritually profound.

However, it's important to note that a Kundalini awakening can also be challenging and intense, as it can bring up repressed emotions and past traumas that need to be healed. It's crucial to approach the Kundalini awakening process with patience, self-care, and the guidance of a qualified spiritual teacher, mentor, or therapist.

Kundalini's awakening in Twin Flames requires preparation, inner work, and a willingness to journey into the depths of oneself. This is when the Divine re-union is experienced when both have done the inner work and healing.

It's a sacred union of their spiritual energies where the merging of their souls creates a surge of intense pleasure and ecstasy that is beyond articulating. At this moment, their energies intertwine and ignite, creating an orgasmic release that goes far beyond the confines of the physical body. It's a blissful and transformative experience that can leave them feeling deeply connected and spiritually awakened. The spiritual orgasm is a unique aspect of the Twin Flames union of their souls and creates a sacred cosmic dance that is beyond the limits of human understanding.

A spiritual orgasm is a divine union of physical and spiritual energies, an experience that goes beyond the physical realm. It's a profound, transcendent connection that goes deep into the core of your being, awakening your soul and expanding your consciousness. With a spiritual orgasm, the pleasure is not solely confined to the body; it's a melding of mind, body, and spirit, an ecstatic fusion of divine energies that can leave you feeling deeply fulfilled and connected on a profound level.

A spiritual orgasmic experience with Twin Flames is common, and just a soft touch, being in each other's presence, can create these energetic orgasms, erotic and intense. They are connected to each other's chakra system and energy centers. When the convergence of Twin Flames happens physically, the divine feminine will send shockwaves through the divine masculine chakras system, triggering an emotionally aroused feeling of pure innocent ecstasy. Bringing him to heights of feelings and dimensions he's never experienced before. This is a divine union, a benevolent union, a holy union, a sacred union. Their divine union is creation itself.

This is what Twin Flames Grace and Michael have been experiencing through these energetic surges of pleasurable energy and spiritual orgasms, as we will see as their story unfolds.

Michaels's Invitation is accepted by Grace for a romantic rendezvous with the man of her dreams. After an enchanting, romantic, magical evening comes to a close, the Twins are now on their way to escape to a secluded and tranquil house tucked away in a private location, the perfect setting for a romantic rendezvous. Nestled amidst lush greenery and surrounded by nature's serenity, this hidden gem offers the ultimate privacy.

As they arrive, they are greeted by a winding path that leads them to the enchanting house, creating a sense of anticipation for the magical, passionate moments ahead. Where nature's secrets whisper delightfully in their ears, and the flames of passion transcend from their sacred heart.

The living area features a roaring fireplace, where the Twins can snuggle up together on a plush sofa while basking in the warm, flickering glow of the fire. They can soak in the bubbling hot tub on the secluded patio under a trillion stars, surrounded by the sounds of nature, unwind together, and immerse themselves in the rejuvenating waters. With the ambiance set and the solace of nature embracing them, these moments will be nothing short of ethereal and magical. Their orgasmic getaway journey together begins in this enchanting haven, where the Twins can intertwine with their love to explode shockwaves of pure unconditional love out into the cosmos.

The Twins' making passionate love is an intimate and transcendent experience, occurring in a carefully chosen, serene setting that allows for deep connection and spiritual intimacy. The emphasis lies not only on the physical act but also on the profound spiritual and emotional bond shared between Twin Flames.

Grace is mesmerized by Michael's romantic planning, and Michael can't stop looking at her beauty and wonder that overcomes her face, making him feel like the luckiest man alive. He takes her by the hand and tells her he'd like to show her something; he takes her to a detached building out behind the house that was a sacred space Michael had created himself.

He says, "I know you like to do yoga and meditate; this is where I find my solitude. I built it myself and am still working on a few things, but this is a special sacred space, and I have dreamed of being here with you as we danced in every dream I've had of us."

Playing a soft melody of serene meditation music, lighting candles, and incense, they faced each other, holding hands and eyes locked; they moved into a sensual slow dance that was familiar with a warm embrace of contentment. Grace and Michael are surrounded by an ambiance of love and enchantment; the Twins embrace the intoxicating atmosphere of their romantic, erotic exploration of creation.

Grace smiles with warmth in her heart and tears of pure exotic bliss and speechlessness from the magnitude of what was happening in this holy sacred moment that she knew was GOD GIFTED.

"I know this melody; we've danced to the same melody in my dreams," Grace said with wonder and childlike eyes.

Michael said, "I know, my love; we were there dancing together to this melody," He said in a sweet and enduring voice. He can't help but lean in for a soft, sweet, sensual kiss, pulling her closer, setting her on his lap, embracing her while nestling his head on her chest. He was hearing palpitations from her racing heart as she wrapped her legs around him, now intertwined, and held each other.

As Grace and Michael continue to anticipate their electrifying union, the energy between them intensifies even further, fuelling a crescendo of erotic bliss that swirls and dances within their bodies. Their souls become entwined in a heavenly symphony of unconditional love, connecting with all this is. The boundaries between heaven and earth cleared.

With hearts pounding and racing, their profound connection pulls them like a magnetic force. The anticipation of their union sends shivers up and down their spines, and they embrace the sheer power of desire that courses through their veins. Their eyes l with pure excitement and passion.

The air is filled with an electric charge, and as they reach the peak of their passion, a palpable energy engulfs them, transcending the boundaries of space and time. In this heightened state of ecstasy, their souls merge, creating an orgasmic explosion of love and light that envelops them with their sacred, innocent, holy, divine love union.

When Twin Flames finally converge physically, it's a potent cocktail of anticipation, desire, and passion that sets their souls ablaze. Their bodies, yearning for the sweet release of ecstasy, both trembling with an electrical current of heightened arousal.

With each touch, their senses ignited, intensifying even more, transcending the boundaries of earthly pleasure.

Their bodies moved in perfect harmony, guided by a shared sense of love and spiritual unity. Every touch and caress sends waves of intense energy through their beings, amplifying their connection. As they explore each other's physical realm, each gesture is filled with tenderness, reverence, and an expression of boundless unconditional love.

In this boundless realm of pleasure, they surrender to the primal urges within, unleashing the raw power of their desires. Every touch, every kiss, is an expression of their deep connection. Every caress is a symphony of sensation, sending waves of pleasure cascading through their beings. Their lips, locked in a fervent dance, taste the sweet essence of longings fulfilled. Their hands explore every curve and contour, forming an undeniable connection, merging their sensuality as their hearts beat in synchrony.

Their lovemaking transcends the physical act itself, becoming their sacred dance in divine union. With every kiss and every caress, they are exchanging passion with mutual recognition of the deep truths hidden within their souls. Their intimate connection goes beyond the physical realm; it becomes a merging of their emotional, mental, and spiritual selves.

When Twin Flames first make love, their physical reactions can vary based on the intensity of their connection and the energy between them. Some common physical manifestations include heightened sensitivity to touch, accelerated heart rate, very emotional bringing them to tears, flushed skin, dilated pupils, and more. The intimate reunion of Twin Flames often generates a profound sense of euphoria and a rush of endorphins, creating a transcendent experience that goes beyond ordinary physical pleasure. The sensations can be overwhelming and deeply passionate as their bodies and souls merge in a fiery dance of desire and connection. It's a truly magical and transformative experience.

As the emotional currents flowed between them, they discovered an unshakable love that seemed to grow with every kiss and every passing moment of erotic pleasure. It was a love that transcended on a multi-dimensional level, a love that had been woven into the fabric of their beings by GOD long before they had the chance to recognize it.

As they lay in each other's arms, they bask in the afterglow of this divine experience, trembling out of control, and it brought them both to tears of bliss and pure ecstasy. They are fully present, savouring the sacred, intense connection they have shared. There is a deep sense of fulfillment and a knowing that they have experienced a cosmic love unlike anything else in existence.

Can you feel the intensity of their convergence, the overwhelming bliss of their sexual ecstasy? It is a moment of profound connection, a culmination of their desires, and a sacred merging of their souls that desire to dance beyond space and time through heaven's gate, just as they did in their heavenly encounters.

Their reunion was nothing short of a cosmic miracle, a supernatural and divine recognition of their intertwined souls, and now they stood reunited in the holy presence of their sacred and divine union. They had found their heaven in each other's embrace.

As they both dozed off in the comfort and completeness of being together, they were awakened by the dawn's light of a new day breaking through the window. They smiled softly at each other, taking in the beauty of the moment. It was as if all their worries had been washed away by the gentle morning sunlight.

Suddenly, they both sat up, staring playfully into each other's eyes. "Who's cooking breakfast?" they both exclaimed in unison, laughing softly at the serendipitous moment. It was a perfect beginning to their perfect day.

After a delightful breakfast, Michael charmingly suggests to Grace that they venture out and embark on a romantic walk through hidden trails. Grace's eyes shimmered with joy as she eagerly accepted his invitation. The prospect of a morning hike with Michael in the serene and peaceful surroundings, where the air was adorned with the sweet scent of flowers and kissed by the morning dew, filled her being with sheer bliss. The mere thought of spending quality time with her beloved in such a tranquil atmosphere caused her heart to dance with anticipation, and her mind conjured vivid images of the picturesque scenery.

Hand in hand, they set off, their steps guided by curiosity and passion, as they explored the breathtaking beauty of the countryside. With every twist and turn down the winding path, their senses were enveloped in the intoxicating fragrance of jasmine and rose petals, adding an alluring touch to their romantically magical.

# Chapter 7
# The Sacred Proposal

The presence of rebirth and new beginnings were bursting through the Twins' with every unison heartbeat. Michael guides Grace on a morning walk to a special location where he has something magically profound planned for her, and he is grateful for his helpful elves. Grace and Michael, wrapped in the magnetism of their connection, embarked on a mesmerizing morning stroll that ignited their senses and set their hearts ablaze. With each step they took, the world around them seemed to unveil its vivid, radiant beauty, captivating them both in a symphony of joy and wonder. Their smiles were a reflection of the exquisite happiness that danced between them.

As if the universe itself conspired to heighten their passion, Michael, with an irresistible glint in his eyes, guided Grace along the winding path to a place that held an essence of magic and destiny for both of them. With a tender gesture, he placed a delicate red piece of yarn that invited her to follow it toward its mysterious destination...

With each gentle tug of the string, an electric current of anticipation surged through Grace's veins, intensifying her desire to uncover the mystery that lay ahead. As they continued their stroll, winding through the path delicately adorned with fragrant rose petals, Grace's heart raced with a potent mixture of excitement and love. Her eyes sparkled with anticipation, mirroring the fervent rhythm of her heartbeat.

As they continued their stroll, the string led them to a path covered with rose petals. Grace, not sure what to think, looked at Michael and smiled with excitement and wonder in her eyes, and her heart beating with a strong, intense feeling of heightened love with this sense of wonder.

As the melody of rushing water grew louder, a crescendo of anticipation filled the air, signaling that their destination was near. Then, a breathtaking clearing emerged before their eyes, revealing a cascading waterfall amidst a picturesque landscape of lush greenery and vibrant flowers. The sight was nothing short of extraordinary, an oasis of beauty that seemed crafted solely for them.

In that perfect moment, surrounded by the ethereal beauty of nature and enshrouded in a palpable aura of love, Grace and Michael locked eyes, sharing an unspoken understanding that this encounter was not simply by chance. It was a testament to their profound connection, a testament to the unyielding power of their desires brought to life.

As the air filled with the intoxicating scent of roses, Michael gently guided Grace toward the center of the heart-shaped formation made of beautiful fresh rose petals. With every step they took, their hearts beat in synchrony as if anticipating the profound moment that was about to unfold.

Feeling the warmth of Michael's hands in hers, Grace's anticipation grew, her pulse quickening with a mix of excitement and nervousness. Then, in a breathtaking gesture, Michael gracefully knelt down on one knee, his eyes locked deeply into hers. At that moment, the world seemed to fade away, leaving only the two of them embraced by a universe of raw emotion.

As tears shimmered in his eyes, mirroring the vulnerability and raw intensity of feelings swirling within him, Michael's charming smile broke through. It was a smile that spoke volumes, carrying an unspoken promise of a love that would transcend time and space. With his voice quivering with excitement and filled with unwavering devotion, he confessed his undying love to Grace, his words like the sweetest melody, echoing within the depths of her heart. At that very moment, he yearned to cherish every second they had together, not willing to waste a single precious moment without her by his side.

"My Love, from the moment our souls intertwined, dancing beyond heaven's gate, I knew that our connection was unlike any other or even knew existed. With you now by my side, I have found a love that is holy, pure, and unconditional. I feel at home when I'm with you, and I can't imagine a future without you. In your presence, I feel a sense of completeness and wholeness that I've never felt before. Our union is a sacred bond and should be honored and treated as such.

Grace, my heart is filled with love and devotion for you. I ask for your hand in marriage as we merge our lives, dreams, and destinies. Together, we will shine brightly as an example of true love by living our lives with love, compassion, and harmony.

My love, in this sacred space, where our souls are nourished by the serenity of our surroundings, I want to take a courageous leap forward and ask you, without reservation or hesitation, to start our sacred journey now." as he pulls out the gorgeous diamond wedding ring, its sparkle, brilliance, with exceptional quality. says "I choose you Grace and I love you from the depth of my heart and soul. Will you marry me?"

With tears of joy in her eyes, Grace gracefully dropped to one knee as well, the air heavy with anticipation; she delicately caressed Michael's face, her touch conveying a potent mixture of desire and affection.

She answers, "Miçhael, darling, according to Heaven, we already are. I am endlessly grateful for a love so electrifyingly beautiful; you and I will bring something extraordinary into each other's lives," giving him a gentle kiss with the intensely pleasurable feeling of deep unconditional love.

Locking her mesmerizing gaze with his, she whispered, "Yes, Michael, I would be honoured to be your wife, sharing and experiencing a love this grand; I love you so much." leaning in for a sweet, soft, sensual kiss.

They envision a future where they will continue to explore the depths of their souls together, creating a life filled with love, passion, and purpose. They will embark on this journey of a lifetime, where every step they take will be infused with the magic of their sacred union.

They poured their hearts out with heartfelt promises of a lifetime of love, companionship, and adventure. Overwhelmed with emotions, tears of happiness and laughter flowed as they embraced, knowing deep within their souls that this proposal was the beginning of a truly captivating journey together.

Their connection deepened as their souls entwined, submerged in an ocean of passion and commitment, and as the world held its breath, time seemed to stand still, allowing the weight of their love to envelop them in a timeless embrace.

As they slowly made their way back towards the house, warm feelings of euphoria enveloped Grace and Michael, their longing for each other now a palpable, captivating force. A renewed sense of connection with one another courses through them, mingling with the intoxicating anticipation of beginning this next chapter of their profound journey, dedicated to contributing to the greater good for their spiritual evolution.

Water, the magical substance that holds immense power, moved in a holy and sacred way as the Twins shared a shower after a life-changing morning. As they stood under the flowing water, their bodies entwined in a fiery embrace, they felt an intense energy surge through them. With each flow of the water, all karmic contracts were broken, cleansing their souls as they let go of all that no longer served their highest good. They felt a profound sense of release as if their past struggles were flowing away with the water, leaving them purified and renewed. It is a sacred dance between two souls, a moment of profound unity and bliss.

The Twins experience spiritual orgasms; it's a divine union of physical and spiritual energies, an experience that goes beyond the physical realm. It's a profound, transcendent connection that goes deep into the core of your being, awakening your soul and expanding your consciousness. With a spiritual orgasm, the pleasure is not solely confined to the body; it's a melding of mind, body, and spirit, an ecstatic fusion of divine energies that can leave you feeling deeply fulfilled and connected on a profound level.

On the other hand, a regular orgasm is a purely physical release of sexual tension, resulting in intense pleasure and a temporary sense of satisfaction. While pleasurable, it is generally focused on the physical sensations without the added depth and spiritual connection.

The flames dance and flicker as the Twins explore each other's bodies, their movements perfectly synchronized. Every touch, every kiss, every caress ignites a fire within them that burns hotter than any flame. In that moment, they are consumed by their desire for each other, lost in the intensity of their lovemaking. It is a moment of pure bliss, where two souls become one, and nothing else in the world matters.

Hot, passionate lovemaking between Twin Flames is a truly magical experience. The cleansing of the water combined with the intense passion between two people who are deeply connected on a soul level creates a powerful energy that electrifies the senses, to put it mildly.

The Twins, eager to celebrate their engagement in a setting that embraced the natural beauty that surrounded them, planned to take the festivities out to the terrace. They longed to lose themselves in the glory of the natural world, allowing the gentle breeze to caress their skin and the moonlight to envelop them in its hypnotic, seductive glow. Together, they would bask in the sensual magic of the world, reveling in the sheer intensity of their connection as they embraced all the delights of nature.

The soft glow of candlelight flickers, casting warm hues upon their faces as they share stories, laughter, and stolen glances. They take in the beauty of the stars as they twinkle and dance through the night sky. The scent of fresh, fragrant wildflowers fills the air while the stillness of the night cocoons them and keeps them safe.

It will be a night to remember, surrounded by the sweet serenades of nature and the love that is shared between them.

In that magical evening, the course of their lives would take a turn as they embark on a new chapter together, exploring uncharted territories of love and devotion, bound by the promise of forever through eternity, experiencing their fulfilling unconditional love for one another.

As the enchanting evening unfolds, Grace and Michael find themselves celebrating their love under the twinkling stars, the magical ambiance heightening their desires. A gentle chill in the air leads them inside, where they find themselves drawn to the inviting warmth of the crackling fireplace. Nestled together, they bask in a cozy and comfortable embrace, their bodies yearning for more. As passion intensifies, their love transcends mere mortal boundaries, unleashing a tempest of powerful emotions that ignite their souls, building towards an exquisite moment of raw, euphoric lovemaking.

Their desires with intense lovemaking in front of the fire certainly set passion ablaze. Imagine the fiery glow illuminating their bodies as they surrender to erotic sensations, their entangled souls merging in a dance of ecstasy. The crackling embers serenaded fervent desires, fuelling their unquenchable thirst for one another. With every touch and embrace, they immerse themselves in holy union, losing themselves to the intoxicating rhythm of their desires. Together, they'll create a blazing inferno of passion that consumes them both, leaving them breathless and infinitely connected in the flames of their insatiable love.

Let's just do it; let's talk about what sex is. Apparently, we've been doing it wrong because it lacks respect and honor. The perception of sex, unfortunately, has been tainted by societal judgments and misunderstood notions. But in truth, it is a profound act that can be elevated to a divine communion with the essence of all that is.

"Holy sacred sex" is the combination of the physical act of sex with spiritual elements. It suggests that intimate connection and sexual pleasure can be transcendent and deeply meaningful when infused with a sense of reverence, respect, and sacredness.

The term "holy" is a state of high esteem, virtuous, and sacred beliefs. "Sacred" refers to something regarded as special, sacred, or worthy of veneration. In truth, it is a profound act that can be elevated to a divine communion with the essence of all that is.

In various religious and spiritual traditions, the concept of holy sacred sex manifests in different ways. It involves setting intentions, being present at the moment, and cultivating mindfulness. Treating each other with love and respect is paramount. Some individuals may incorporate additional elements such as prayer, meditation, or invoking spiritual guidance to deepen the spiritual connection in this intimate dance.

It's crucial to recognize that the definition of holy, sacred sex may vary based on personal beliefs and individual interpretations of spirituality. However, at its core, it is an expression of deep connection and reverence for the divine energy that flows within us and between us.

Your understanding and appreciation of the sacredness of sex should be known as a truly beautiful experience. It's a reminder that we can reclaim and honour the profound magnificence of this act of holy convergence.

It is the expression of unconditional love.

# Chapter 8
# Divine Purpose

It is believed that the divine reunification and harmonization of Twin Flames can create a ripple effect of love, healing, and transformation throughout society and the universe. Twin Flames are seen as catalysts for positive change, inspiring others to awaken to their true selves and align with a higher consciousness.

The path of Twin Flames involves a deeper level of spiritual growth and understanding. Their purpose involves a process of spiritual awakening or enlightenment where they become more aware of their true nature and the interconnectedness to all things.

It is important to note that everyone's path is authentic, and being a Twin Flame does not necessarily dictate a predetermined path. Each individual has their own lessons and challenges to work through, and the path of Twin Flames can vary greatly from person to person.

As the Twins, Grace and Michael, stirred awake, still aroused from the heavenly enchanted weekend, and on their first Sunday morning waking up together, they were enveloped in the sense of warmth, profound connection, and deep satisfied pleasure.

"Good morning, Michael," Grace greeted him with a radiant smile. "To see your handsome face first thing in the morning makes my heart skip a beat. You give me butterflies in my heart."

Michael chuckled in delight, his eyes fixed on Grace. "Oh, my love, it truly is a perfect morning, and we're just beginning this beautiful journey together. When I opened my eyes and saw your breathtaking face, it unleashed a swarm of goose bumps all over me. You truly have me spellbound."

Their laughter mingled as they mingled more with shared excitement and morning kisses, filling the room with unbridled affection and playfulness.

They began their day sitting together in perfect harmony, meditating on the evolution of their own personal growth while still trying to grasp the grand magnitude of what was happening to them. They were delightful, to say the least. Through the practices of mindfulness, self-reflection, and meditation, they continued to deepen their spiritual bond and align themselves with their soul's purpose, emerging from this sacred space feeling renewed and whole.

Twins may feel a strong calling to seek knowledge and understanding of the deeper truths of existence, questioning societal norms and seeking a higher purpose in life. Twin Flames often have a deep sense of compassion and empathy for others and a deep feeling that they are responsible for their positive contribution to the world.

Grace and Michael truly have hearts of gold. As they embark on their mission to make a positive impact on the world, their souls brim with passion and purpose. They unveil the realization that their true calling is to provide healing and compassion to those in need. With boundless love and a profound understanding of the significance of caring for others, they are determined to teach the world the importance of assisting others as humanitarians and assisting the return of humanity back to their true nature, which is the state of love and joy.

With boundless love and a profound understanding of the significance of caring for others, they are determined to set the example of the importance of assisting others as humanitarians and the importance of being good stewards of Mother Earth.

Together, they will intertwine their souls' purpose, spreading warmth and kindness wherever they go. Making a profound impact on their journey and what it will have on the lives they touch. It's a beautiful and noble mission.

The Twins' are here to assist humanity's evolution and seek to create a more sustainable, balanced, and harmonious society through self-sustaining knowledge within individual communities. We are at a great time of unlearning these old patterns that have been forced upon humanity. However, love is back in full force, armed with the unconditional love of all that is, and that love is here to stay and flourish to bring in New Earth. In a happy world, expressing love for one another it's the unlearning of fear that will allow love to enter the heart of humanity.

As the afternoon unfolded, Grace and Michael found themselves engrossed in a captivating exchange of ideas centered around Grace's visionary dream of establishing global healing centers. Their voices carried the sweet melody of affection and deep-seated respect that can only be shared between Twin Flames.

Twin Flames are believed to have traversed through countless lifetimes, accumulating a wealth of wisdom and profound insights along the way. This profound journey often imbues them with extraordinary qualities, including heightened empathy, an innate intuition, and an insatiable longing for genuine spiritual connection.

Additionally, Twin Flames contribute to the collective evolution of humanity by embodying and spreading love, compassion, empathy, and understanding through Christ's consciousness. Their union is viewed as a powerful force that can elevate humanity's collective consciousness,

Depending on their personal beliefs, some common perspectives suggest that they are here to guide others, to bring balance and harmony to the world, and to continue their own spiritual growth and evolution. Ultimately, the purpose of Twin Flames, like any other individual, is to find meaning and fulfillment in their own unique journey to discover their authentic self through experiences of life. Twins possess a deep wisdom and maturity beyond their years. They are a powerful force of love connected to all that is, and they know it.

As the day wore on, Grace opened up to Michael about a charity fundraiser she and Emma had planned and coordinated, with all proceeds going towards financing the establishment of much-needed healing centers.

"It's an open invitation, Michael. I would be honoured if you joined me to celebrate such a special and noble cause," Grace proposed with a warm smile. Michael, taking her hand in his, leaned in and planted a tender kiss on her palm. "I wouldn't miss it for the world, my love. Your selfless, admirable intentions show me the true depth of your beautiful heart," he said with conviction, his eyes ablaze with an undeniable passion. "I accept, Grace," he added softly, pulling her into a tight embrace as they both basked in the warmth and excitement of their shared purpose.

Grace showed Michael the blueprint plan for the healing centers; Michael, being an engineer, knew exactly what he was looking at.

"We want communities to learn to self-sustain through growing their own food and learn many different practices to enrich daily life and health. Providing the most advanced technologies to heal at a cellular level, with each center providing its own energy with no outside sources needed. Logistics is not an issue; they can be built anywhere since they are sustainable with the production of their own energy needed to operate.

Sharing her blueprint plan for the healing centers, Grace watched with excitement as Michael, a skilled engineer, deftly analysed every detail. "Grace, these plans are fantastic, and allowing the communities to govern their own center and energy is genius," he exclaimed. "Your idea to empower communities to govern their own center is truly admirable."

As their discussion continued, Grace elaborated on her vision for the healing centers - a place where local communities can cultivate their own food, learn various practices to enhance and enrich daily life and health and benefit from cutting-edge cellular-level healing technologies. The sheer passion and intensity in their voices left no doubt in their minds that this was the very beginning of something truly extraordinary.

Excited for this divine purpose, their hearts beating like a symphony, the last evening of their unforgettable rendezvous has just begun. As they sat down for a candlelit dinner, the soft flickering glow and the warmth of the fire created an intimate ambiance that perfectly matched the depth of their connection. In each other's embrace, their souls entwined, finding solace and pure contentment.

The convergence of Twin Flames reunited as one is a breathtaking dance of destiny. With every touch, every gentle caress, their desires stirred like a tempestuous storm, unleashing a torrent of passion that had been building between them for lifetimes. Their bodies moved in perfect harmony, entangled in a dance that spoke of love, longing, and sweet surrender.

Overcome with reluctance to part from each other and return to their individual work responsibilities, Grace and Michael came to a mutual decision - they would extend their lovers' rendezvous for one more night until Monday evening and use the extra time to catch up on work and plan for the week ahead.

Time seemed to stand still as they relished in the beauty of their divine reunion. With every shared glance, their eyes revealed a sacred truth, a knowing that they were meant to be together for this divine purpose. Their connection was more than physical; it was a fusion of their souls, a divine bond that transcended earthly limitations beyond the human mind's comprehension.

In the quiet moments between whispered words and stolen kisses, their desires grew even stronger. The air was saturated with their intoxicating arousal, heightening their senses with pleasure. Through their tender exploration, the depths of their ecstasy reach the pinnacle of their desires.

As the night wore on, the flame of their passion burned brighter, igniting an insatiable hunger that could only be quenched by the culmination of their desires. With hearts pounding and bodies intertwined, they surrendered to the irresistible pull of their shared destiny, embracing the magic that unfolded between them.

As the dawn approached, they basked in the afterglow, their bodies blissfully spent and their souls forever ignited. In their final moments together, they knew that this evening had marked the beginning of their timeless love story, a story written in the stars and sealed with unbreakable sacred vows.

"Michael, this time we've spent together has felt truly heavenly and magical," Grace expressed with deep gratitude. Michael responded, "I love you immensely, my darling, and I believe we are destined for a lifetime of love with our divine, purposeful mission.

"Shall we go now, my love?" he asked, "No, Michael," she pouted playfully, her bottom lip jutting out in the cutest of ways. He embraced her tightly, assuring her that their time together would never truly end and that they would soon be back to this erotic solitude they had found in the divine convergence of their souls.

Reluctantly, Michael accompanied Grace back home, not wanting to part from her for even a moment. However, Grace had obligations to attend to, such as preparing for the upcoming fundraiser with event planner and best friend Emma, who was expected to arrive this week. The passing of each day seemed to slow down as the Twins eagerly anticipated seeing each other, the ache of longing to be together.

Later, Grace received a message from Emma confirming her safe arrival home. Grace immediately called her to arrange their dress fittings and to plan a much-needed catch-up lunch for the next day — a chance to reconnect and share the exciting developments in each of their lives.

Emma and Grace met for lunch the following day to exchange stories and finalize details for the upcoming fundraiser event.
As the two friends basked in the shared intimacy of their confessions, a wave of empowerment washed over Grace. She realized that she was not alone in her pursuit of a love that stirred her soul and awakened her senses. The knowledge that Emma, her dear friend, had also experienced the intoxicating allure of romance and this desire fueled Grace's determination to embrace her own yearning for Michael with feelings of great intensity of warm and steady emotion, unabashed fervor.

Grace's voice trembled slightly as she spoke, her words dripping with a mix of longing and passion, mirroring the electric energy that coursed through her veins. Emma watched, captivated by

Grace's story, sensing the intensity of her desire and the profound connection she had found in Michael, the man in/ her dreams.

In that moment, as they continued to exchange stories and revelled in the depths of their desires, Grace and Emma forged an unspoken bond, united by their shared understanding of their new love's passion that enveloped both of their lives. They both knew that true fulfillment did not come from holding back but from embracing their desires and surrendering to the throes of unbridled passion; Emma has supported Grace from the beginning of this calling.

And so, as they left the restaurant, their hearts ablaze with the fire of their newfound untamed desires, Grace and Emma vowed to support each other on their respective journeys towards love and fulfillment of their divine purposes.

The stakes couldn't be higher for this fundraiser, which is needed to catapult their vision of global healing centers into production.

# Chapter 9
# Uniting for a Cause

In a world where compassion and empathy are often overshadowed by the hustle and bustle of daily life, it is heartwarming to witness a night of fundraising that brings people together for a common cause. Such an event not only raises funds for worthy organizations or projects but also serves as a reminder of the power of unity and collective action.

Invitation: *"You are cordially invited to a fundraiser at the historic opera house downtown on 11/11 at 8 PM. The event aims to raise funds for the production of the first-of-its-kind, community-governed healing centers on a global scale. There will be a renowned chef-catered dinner, musical performances by well-known musicians, and other attractions to enjoy.*

*We hope to see you there!"*

The gem of a venue was planned to host the fundraiser. The venue is a luxurious opera house decorated with gold, ornate furniture, and marble floors with intricate patterns. A grand chandelier hangs above the lobby, casting light and shadow over the room. The walls have a red velvet backdrop with golden trim, and there is a sweeping staircase leading up to a box. The stage is surrounded by rows of plush seats, and a fancy red curtain covers the stage. The venue is designed to allow for fundraising events, with enough space for dinner and dancing and the ability to host musical performances.

As the sun sets and the stars begin to twinkle in the night sky, a sense of excited anticipation fills the air. Volunteers, donors, and supporters gather at a grand venue adorned with colorful banners and decorations, all in the spirit of giving. The atmosphere is electric, buzzing with excitement, and a shared commitment to making a difference in the world.

As Michael arrived to pick up Grace, the anticipation between them crackled in the air with electricity. It's been days since the Twins last saw each other. Michael was dressed impeccably in a sleek black and white tuxedo. With every step he took, his confidence radiated, setting the stage for an unforgettable night.

Then there was Grace, standing before him like a goddess. Her choice of gown was nothing short of divine. She captivated Michael's gaze, wearing an intoxicating Shoulder Elegant Ruffle Trim Bodycon Dress in a deep shimmering green that perfectly accentuated her curves. Every ruffle seemed to whisper promises of a tantalizing encounter that awaited them both. Her hair cascaded down in luscious waves, its natural beauty enhanced by a touch of subtle shimmer. It flowed with a captivating grace, framing her face and drawing attention to her mesmerizing eyes, which mirrored the promise of passion and desire that danced in the depths of her soul.

As they arrived at the fundraiser and stood together, they were the embodiment of a power couple, and the world seemed to pause in awe. At that moment, all eyes were drawn to them, unable to resist the magnetic pull of their undeniable chemistry. Their presence exuded a tantalizing blend of confidence and sensuality, leaving no doubt that they were embarking on a night that would redefine the limits of their heart's desires. The night is ripe with possibilities, and they are ready to embark on a journey where passion knows no bounds.

When they step into the beautifully adorned hall, they are enveloped by a sense of warmth and optimism. There were bubbling conversations and joyous laughter as guests donned their elegant attire and gathered to support an important cause. The room is adorned with shimmering lights and vibrant decorations, casting an enchanting glow that matches the excitement in the air. As you make your way through the crowd, you can't help but be touched by the genuine smiles and heartfelt conversations that fill every corner.

Grace, in her role as the radiant hostess, occupied center stage, exuding an aura of warmth and grace to welcome all those who gathered in support of a profoundly noble mission - to selflessly care for others. The passion that burned within her was not limited to the depths of her desires but also extended to a fervent dedication to making a positive impact on the world around her.

"Ladies and gentlemen,

Good evening, and welcome to this extraordinary gathering in support of our beloved project, which aims to establish free healing centers worldwide. I am deeply honored to stand before you tonight as the hostess of this meaningful fundraiser, and I cannot express enough gratitude for your presence and generous contributions. Your unwavering support has propelled us closer to realizing our vision of communities where healing and hope thrive, where happiness and wellness become the norm.

Tonight, we gather not only to celebrate the remarkable vision that has been transformed into reality but also to acknowledge with deep appreciation the unwavering commitment of our remarkable community and the boundless generosity of our esteemed donors. It is a privilege to stand here, representing our shared mission, and I am filled with an overwhelming sense of pride and gratitude.

Together, we are making a profound difference in the lives of countless individuals, creating a legacy of compassion and healing that will resonate for generations to come. Your presence here tonight is a testament to the power of community and the capacity we have to create positive change.

Let us continue to shine the light of hope into the darkest corners of despair, embracing the belief that everyone deserves access to healing, love, and support. Thank you for your unwavering dedication to this cause, and thank you for joining us on this remarkable journey.

May this evening be a testament to our collective commitment to fostering a world where healing knows no boundaries.

"Thank you."

As the evening progresses, the program begins, and the atmosphere shifts to one of inspiration and motivation. Speakers take the stage, sharing personal stories and rallying attendees to join hands in making a difference. Their words resonate deeply, igniting a fire within each guest to do their part in creating positive change. Their stories stimulate their curiosity, leaving them wanting to learn more about the organization and the individuals they have impacted.

Firstly, having self-sustaining living experts to oversee certain aspects of the plan ensures that we will be equipped with the knowledge and skills to live independently and harmoniously with the environment. These experts will help us establish sustainable practices such as organic farming, permaculture, and alternative energy sources, ensuring that they will confidently and responsibly meet the community's needs with free energy powering each center.

Growing your own food holds immense importance in one's journey towards self-reliance. By communities cultivating their own crops, they gain control over the quality and nutritional value of what is consumed. It also fosters a profound connection with the Earth and a sense of fulfillment and satisfaction in nurturing and seeing the fruits of their labor flourish.

Now, let's talk about healing med beds that operate on a cellular level. These advanced technologies have the incredible ability to promote healing and regeneration within the body. Imagine being able to lay on a healing med bed and experience cellular rejuvenation, accelerated recovery, and overall enhanced well-being. These beds hold the potential to revolutionize our approach to healthcare, providing non-invasive and highly effective healing solutions.

Lastly, guidance for the spiritual growth of individuals and communities is vital for fostering a sense of interconnectedness and oneness. This spiritual guidance helps individuals explore their inner depths, awaken their higher selves, and find purpose and meaning in life. It also promotes unity within communities, cultivating empathy, love, and understanding among individuals.

These elements combine to create a harmonious and thriving environment to live in. They form the foundation of a fulfilling and holistic lifestyle, allowing them to flourish both physically and spiritually.

The evening wouldn't be complete without a touch of elegance and entertainment. The music playing at the fundraiser is a captivating blend of rhythmic beats and soulful melodies that effortlessly fill the air. The lively tunes create an atmosphere of celebration and joy, captivating the audience and making them tap their feet in sync with the rhythm. The talented vocals and stirring instrumentals evoke a range of emotions, from nostalgia to gratitude, as attendees sway along to the music's intoxicating celebratory flow.

With its diverse repertoire, the music seamlessly transitions from upbeat and energetic tunes that ignite a sense of unity and togetherness to soul-stirring ballads that touch the hearts of those present. Ultimately, the music at this fundraiser elevates the ambiance, creating an unforgettable experience that leaves the crowd buzzing with excitement and a renewed sense of purpose.

Michael found himself captivated by Joseph, the original engineer who had meticulously crafted the blueprints for the global healing centers. A magnetic connection formed between them, fueled by their shared academic background at a prestigious engineering university.

As their conversation unfolded, Michael discovered an unexpected surge through him, his mind simultaneously consumed by thoughts of Grace and the intimate connections he yearned to forge with her. The night beckoned to him, promising a journey of unbridled passion and romance, intensified by Grace's noble vision of caring for others by making a profound impact.

With this exhilarating rush and the electrifying conversations shared with Joseph, Michael eagerly embraced the moment with Grace, his heart overflowing with anticipation for their divine purpose together. As they stood there, their destinies intertwined, they eagerly looked forward to the night that lay ahead—a night that would bind their love and purpose into a single, glorious entity.

"Grace, my beloved, I am immensely proud of you. Your actions tonight were truly admirable," Michael exclaimed, his voice brimming with affection. "Will you bless me with a dance, my love?"

Overwhelmed by the sheer beauty of the moment, Grace couldn't hold back her emotions. "Thank you, my dear. I would be honored to dance with you," she replied, her voice trembling with happiness. "This evening has surpassed all expectations. With the funds we've raised, we can now break ground and begin building our first healing centers. I'm overjoyed that you are here to celebrate this special night with me, Michael. The entire evening has been such a success."

As the night drew to a close, their hearts full and spirits soaring, they bid farewell to the remaining guests at the fundraiser, ready

to embark on their journey together, hand-in-hand, towards a
future built of their sacred love and divine purpose.

# Chapter 10
# Breaking Ground

What a truly magnificent night it was at the fundraiser. Grace's heart brimmed with a potent mix of excitement and relief as she revelled in the success of the event. Now, the Twins have returned to Grace's home, a place of comfort and intimacy, where they could celebrate this significant milestone on their shared journey towards this divine mission.

With Michael and his company now fully on board with Joseph, their united vision of creating the very first self-sustaining healing center was about to become a reality. The excitement bubbled within them both, knowing that come Monday morning, they would be breaking ground and embarking on the profound production of this healing sanctuary, setting the stage for community-governed healing centers.

They were nestled cosily beside the crackling fireplace, a warm glow dancing in their eyes as they savoured the unity and the exquisite flavors of the wine in their glasses. Memories of the magical night at the successful fundraiser filled their minds, intertwining with the electrical current that pulsed between them, heightening the allure and arousal of the present moment.

"My love," Grace said with tears of joy, "this dream I've nurtured for so long came about through my own healing process, and to see this is unfolding into something bigger than I envisioned and now playing out right before my eyes, like a breathtaking masterpiece, with you by my side supporting it's revealing to me a greater promise than I could've imagined.

We collaborate to construct this extraordinary space, a haven of healing and nurturing for the community's caring and compassion for one another. Michael, I can hardly contain the excitement and fulfillment. Are you feeling the same exhilaration as I am for what lies ahead? Because this is big."

 Michael replied, "Absolutely, more than I can express my love. This passionate cause goes above and beyond just the ground-breaking of a center; it's a movement for healing individuals that will heal the world. You are right; it's big."
Joseph and I saw that the plans to construct the centers should be fairly simple to produce in masses with ease. This is very exciting, Grace. I thought we could take a Sunday drive to the site; I'd love to see it before we meet up with the team."

This is the purpose of Twin Flames; they are serving a greater mission. Grace and Michael will be inseparable; now, with the clarity of their divine purpose together, they will be an unstoppable force. The true purpose of Twin Flames is to assist in moulding others into the type of persons who are capable of embodying divine, unconditional love and the sacredness of the two becoming one… first for themselves and then for humanity.

When Twin Flames reunite, it's not just to bring their own soul back into alignment as divine love. They are also here to assist others to do the same. They are here for the greater good of all. They are here to fulfil a mission beyond their own personal development and aid the spiritual revolution as humanity awakening from a mind control coma on the planet.

The Twins had orchestrated a Sunday drive to the sacred location, where their now shared dream would be produced into a blissful reality, like a vision unveiled before their very eyes. The Twins embarked on a picturesque drive to the breathtaking site on what can only be described as a perfect day. The gentle breeze swirled around them as they pulled up to the sprawling property, and from the first step out of the car, they both seemed to be enveloped in a sense of mystique. The lush green field, with its mesmerizing surroundings of towering trees, seemed to exude almost magical energy, captivating their senses and drawing them further into its enchanting embrace.

Their eyes were irresistibly drawn to the captivating sight atop the cliffs, which appeared to be a magnificent castle nestled among the verdant landscape. As they wandered through the property, a sense of wonder and awe washed over them, as if the very spirit of the place was weaving its spell upon their shared heart and soul. Each step they took seemed to deepen their connection with this ethereal place, leaving them both spellbound by its beauty and secrets.

Eager to unveil the mysteries that awaited them, they embarked on a captivating drive towards the enigmatic castle perched majestically atop the cliffs. As they pulled up to the entrance, it was as if they had stumbled upon a fairy tale come to life. The castle, with its timeless grandeur and captivating allure, exuded an aura of romance and regality that left them both breathless. They discovered that the castle was renowned for hosting grand weddings and glamorous events, adding an extra layer of allure to their already exhilarating exploration. The Twins were drawn into a world where dreams seemed to intertwine with reality, and the air was filled with an irresistible sense of enchantment and wonder.

They yearned to wander the exquisite grounds and soak in more of the enchanting scenery, being led by a captivating event planner. Stepping through the lobby adorned with a magnificent chandelier at its heart, they followed the planner outside, where Grace and Michael gazed out over the valley, the very site where the healing center was taking shape. The planner, in awe of the picturesque view, mentioned how it would be perfect for outdoor weddings. As they conversed, Grace couldn't help but share her heartfelt connection to the healing center below.

On their way back, a playful smile danced upon Grace's lips as she turned to Michael, her voice laced with desire. "Michael," she whispered softly, "You know I long to feel your presence by my side every day. Would you like to stay at my place as our connection deepens through the magic of this blessed production?" Michael's eyes sparkled with desire as he responded, his voice filled with anticipation, "Grace, my love, that thought has consumed my mind. Let us stop by my apartment to gather what I need, and then we can surrender to the tantalizing passion of loving each other every single day." As he took her hand in his with a tender kiss that ignited a fire within them both.

Their eagerness intensified, their bodies humming with anticipation as they embraced the warmth and intimacy of another unforgettable evening together. They couldn't wait to pick up right where they left off the night before, their passionate embrace illuminated by the flickering flames of the fireplace, transcending them to a beautiful soul dance beyond heaven's gate. Everything is falling into place beautifully with divine timing.

On a crisp Monday morning, the Twins eagerly convened with Joseph and the rest of the dedicated team at the serene site, their hearts brimming with fervent determination to orchestrate the realization of a beautiful dream. As the team ready to assemble, Joseph warmly expressed his gratitude to each member for their unwavering commitment. In a poignant gesture, he presented Grace with a gleaming new shovel, a symbol of commencement and empowerment. With a sense of honour and purpose, he entrusted her with the pivotal task of breaking ground and initiating the birth of this extraordinary vision of the healing centers she envisioned so long ago during her own healing process.

Grace, her spirit ablaze with passion and gratitude, accepted the symbolic tool with grace and humility. "Of course," she replied, her voice resonating with determination and sincerity. "And I must add that each and every one of us has poured our hearts and souls into this endeavour from its inception. While this dream may have sprung from my heart's desire, it has flourished and thrived because of our collective dedication and tireless efforts. It is not just my dream; it is our dream."

Tears of profound gratitude and unrestrained joy cascaded down Grace's cheek, a poignant testament to the depth of her emotions and the magnitude of this shared achievement. Standing proudly by Grace's side, Michael gazed at her with an overwhelming sense of admiration and adoration, intimately intertwined with a surge of pride for the phenomenal woman he was fortunate enough to call his beloved.

The first shovel has broken ground, and Grace is not able to control her tears of joy and the awe of the dream coming to fruition; it has indeed been a process.

This remarkable group of experts is poised to craft an Eco-friendly haven, utilizing sustainable materials and energy-efficient design to harmonize with the environment. The integration of renewable energy sources, such as solar panels and wind turbines, promised to permeate the center with a sustainable power that transcended the limitations of traditional energy sources.

This will encourage communities to be involved and collaborate through volunteering, events, and partnerships to operate the centers at no cost to those who are in need of healing and good maintenance for self-care. The teachings of the importance of being good stewards of the earth by caring for lush, bountiful organic gardens that not only provide an abundance of fresh, wholesome produce for nourishing meals but also promote the empowering notion of self-sustainability.

Imagine wandering through a healing space that beckons you to explore, offering serene meditation rooms, enchanting yoga studios, cosy therapy spaces, and delightful outdoor areas where you can reconnect with the raw beauty of nature. Immerse yourself in a world of holistic healing where a diverse range of modalities such as acupuncture, reiki, and the curative power of herbal medicine effortlessly stir your senses.

Expanding one's knowledge through captivating educational workshops and classes, exploring sustainable living, embracing the art of healthy eating, diving into the depths of mindfulness, and indulging in other self-improvement topics. Here, mindfulness and self-care practices are cherished, with opportunities to engage in blissful meditation, invigorating breathwork, and soul-stirring mindfulness exercises that nurture your innate healing system.

Not stopping there, picture the game-changing advanced medical devices infused with ground-breaking quantum technology, uniquely designed to heal and rejuvenate the body, awakening a vibrant vitality within.

With unwavering determination and an unwavering spirit, they worked tirelessly to bring their vision to life. As weeks flew by, their collective efforts took the shape of a remarkable healing center that stood as a beacon of hope for the community. It thrived on the principles of sustainability, blending innovative technologies with ancient wisdom and promising transformative experiences for all who sought solace within its walls.

With every detail meticulously planned and every obstacle conquered, the center now stood as a testament to their unwavering dedication and shared passion. Yet, their journey was far from over. With the foundational groundwork laid down, the time had come to embark on the next phase - the training of the community's ambassadors by skilled technicians in the art of utilizing the center's advanced healing technologies.

It was a venture that spoke to the core of their beings, a chance to empower others with the knowledge and wisdom they had so passionately embraced. Grace and Michael knew that this phase was crucial in ensuring the center's longevity and impact on the community at large. With eagerness and anticipation dancing in their eyes, they prepared to pass on the torch of their profound knowledge, igniting a flame of transformative healing that would radiate far beyond the confines of this healing center itself.

In the span of four mesmerizing months, Grace and Michael found themselves in a state of their convergent souls, inseparable as they embarked on a passionate journey to launch the first-ever self-sustainable healing center.

Their hearts and souls were intricately fused, fueling not only their own desires but also serving as a vivacious driving force for the entire team involved. The shared excitement that pulsed through their veins was infectious, capturing the hearts of each individual who had joined them on this exhilarating endeavor.

Today, the community is gathering with friends and family who will join Grace and the teams for the ribbon-cutting ceremony of this dream come true, this vision fulfilled. Setting in motion powerful energy that radiates throughout the universe through heavenly space, sending pure galactic love to wherever it is needed, its powerful energy has the ability to raise the vibrational energy anywhere.

Grace would start with a few words.

"Ladies and gentlemen,

Good Morning,

I am honored to be standing before you today as we celebrate the grand opening of our first self-sustaining healing center. This day marks a significant moment for us as we officially open the doors to the public and embark on a new chapter in not only our own personal healing journey but also humanity's healing journey.

I would like to express my deepest gratitude to all of you who have joined us for this momentous occasion. Your presence here today is a testament to the support and encouragement that we have received throughout this process. We are truly grateful for your unwavering support.

The establishment of the healing center has been a labor of love, dedication, and hard work. It has been a dream that has come to fruition through the collaborative efforts of many individuals. I would like to extend my heartfelt appreciation to all those who have contributed to making this day a reality. From our dedicated team, who have poured their passion into ensuring that every detail is perfect, to our supporters and donors, who have believed in our vision and provided us with the necessary resources to bring it to life, we are immensely grateful for your contributions.

As we stand here today, ready to cut this ribbon and officially declare the center officially open, we are filled with a profound sense of excitement and anticipation for the future. A sustainable healing center is more than just a physical space; it is a place where healing and being joyful, where friendships and connections will be formed, and daily lives will be enriched.

Our goal was to make a positive impact in the lives of those who walk through these doors, and we are determined to leave a lasting legacy that extends far beyond the confines of these walls.

Thank you once again for your presence here today. We look forward to the adventures that lie ahead, and we are grateful for the opportunity to share them with each and every one of you.

Without further ado, it is my honor to declare the Spiritual Bloom Healing Center officially open! Thank you."

The ribbon has been officially cut and is open for business.

# Chapter 11
# Amazing Grace

After finishing the ribbon-cutting ceremony for the grand opening, giving tours, and sharing information about the healing center, it was time to celebrate. Michael had something very special planned to celebrate this milestone: a celebration party for friends, family, the teams, and donors who had contributed to bringing their shared accomplishments to fruition. The event was to be held at the majestic castle overlooking the center.

Grace had no idea that Michael had been planning an event since the inception of the production of the healing center. With Emma's support, Michael had orchestrated a grand surprise— a wedding for Grace. The magnitude of the impending surprise was unfathomable to Grace, and it was risky, but Emma and Grace's mother were not only present to celebrate the dream healing center opening but also to assist in making this magical evening come to life for Grace and Michael.

The rich and luxurious ballroom at the historic Castle is adorned with cascading crystal chandeliers, casting a warm, romantic glow over the entire space. The walls are draped in luxurious gold and ivory fabrics, creating an atmosphere of regal sophistication. A rich tapestry of fragrant blooms - luscious roses, peonies, and orchids - adorns every surface, infusing the air with a floral perfume.

Out on the terrace, a wedding ceremony was coming to life. The aisle leads to a breathtaking floral arch overflowing with blooms in every shade of pink and ivory, with the makings to compliment an enchanting wedding. As Grace arrived, she was stricken when she noticed the perfect color palette of the wedding decorations out on the terrace, the same color palette she'd planned since she was a little girl and she had chosen for her very own dream wedding.

As the guests began to arrive, Michael gently took Grace by the hand and whispered, "Walk with me, Grace," as he offered his arm for her to take. Together, they made their way to the terrace on the cliff overlooking the illuminated healing center. In a softly stirring voice, Michael confessed to Grace that he had meticulously planned the wedding of their dreams. "Grace, my love, the wedding taking shape is for our wedding for our sacred union." His words wrapped around her like a warm embrace, evoking a potent mixture of wonder, love, and sheer delight within her. As the realization sank in that this entire spectacle had been orchestrated solely for their sacred union.

Grace's eyes widened, and tears of joy cascaded down her cheeks, mingling with a radiant smile that graced her lips. "How...how did you manage all of this?" Grace asked, her words faltering as she struggled to comprehend the scale of Michael's heartfelt gesture.

With a reassuring and loving gaze, Michael replied, "My dearest Grace, everything you need is waiting for you in your very own luxurious bridal suite. A curated rack of exquisite wedding dresses awaits your choosing, and an expert hair and makeup professional is ready to transform you into the stunning bride you've always dreamed of."

The shock on Grace's face gradually transformed into a radiant mixture of disbelief and euphoria. She couldn't fathom the lengths Michael went to make this evening a fairy-tale come true, and it had Emma written all over it. Overwhelmed with gratitude, she hugged him tightly, unable to find the perfect words to express her love and appreciation. In this moment, all worries and uncertainties vanished, swept away by the wave of passion and devotion that defined their connection. Their journey to this point had been filled with longing and longing deferred, and now, the stage was set for a night of unbridled passion and a grand celebration of their profound, sacred love.

Michael escorted Grace to her bridal suite. "Grace, I love you with all my heart, and I hope this is alright. I want to give you something magical to celebrate your accomplishments and dedication, as well as celebrate our beautiful love. With our travels, I wasn't sure we'd have time, and I don't want another moment to go by without you being my wife." She smiled, giving Michael a kiss of acceptance and gratitude. "Michael, this is so romantic. You're just the best person, and I love you. My heart is overflowing with unbound love for you, so much so that I am marrying you today. Even though according to Heaven, we already are."

She enters the bridal suite, and her Mother and Emma are there waiting to assist her with all her needs for her grand wedding. Emma and Grace have talked about this day in detail since childhood. Hair and makeup were present with none other than the enigmatic magician of fashion, Toni. With every skilful stroke of his brush, her face bright and glowing, Toni superbly transformed Grace into the stunning bride she was born to be.

As she said yes to the dress with the support and input from her mother, Emma, and Toni, she stood there looking in the mirror; she never looked so radiantly beautiful, all of them with dropped jaws and tears of joy at the sight of Grace as an enchanted bride.

She stands with undeniable elegance, her figure draped in a radiant gown, glistening sequins tracing delicate patterns along the fabric. Upon her head rests a crown with a veil fit for a queen, a dazzling masterpiece crafted from pure gold, encrusted with a symphony of precious gemstones that catch the light and cast a mesmerizing aura around her. Each jewel was chosen to reflect her regal allure and radiant spirit. Every movement she makes sends ripples of glowing beauty through the air. She is adorned with sparkling bright jewels that glimmer with every gesture. This night has truly been blessed with the magic of divine sacred love.

Grace's mother takes her daughter's hands whilst tearing up more and says, "Grace, I don't have a word to express the vision of beauty you are and all the proud feelings I am experiencing on this special day of yours. I am so proud of you and very happy for you. If only your father could be here, he would be so proud of you, Grace." She takes her daughter by both hands and says, "I know exactly what he would say to his daughter so dear to his heart on her wedding day, and the accomplishment with a dream fulfilled that you brought to fruition by following your father's guidance wholeheartedly.

He would say, 'Do all you do with your whole heart because I love you with my whole heart. You are my sweet daughter, and your happiness is what fills my heart.' You were always daddy's girl, and he loved you so much, as did I." He gave her a blessed kiss on Grace's forehead, adding, "We both knew you would do amazingly profound things with your life. Why do you think we named you Grace? You are our amazing Grace." That moved Grace's heart through the devoted love from both her parents and her mother expressing it.

It was time. As Grace came through the double doors to the terrace, all eyes were fixated on the vision of a stunning bride before them. As she exuded a radiant aura, her beauty was amplified by bright sparks of recognition and pure joy. Her heart swells with appreciation for her parents, friends, and loved ones for their unwavering love and encouragement that has made this remarkable day possible.

Michael stands in awe as his bride enters the terrace, feeling as if he's extremely blessed with the lovely vision of his bride and divine counterpart, tears welling up in his eyes as he takes in the breathtaking sight of his incredible bride - the other half of his sacred heart and soul. His pulse quickens; he undoubtedly feels a primal magnetism towards her. As she glides down the aisle, every step radiates an irresistible allure, an embodiment of sensuality and fiery passion.

The sight of her beautiful presence fills Michael's heart with pure joy. Her presence makes him feel a surge of emotions as he embraces the vulnerability that overcomes him. He lets the tears flow freely, and they stream down his face with a testament to the overwhelming feelings of their holy love that fills his heart.

Their gazes lock, electricity crackling between them, creating an invisible web of holy desire that envelops the entire space. At that moment, time stands still as they are both fully aware of the profound connection they share - a connection that transcends the physical, intertwining their souls in an eternal dance of unwavering, unconditional love.

Grace experiences an emotional surge through her veins, making her feel overwhelmed as she glides down the aisle, her heart bursting with pleasurable joy. She feels a radiant warmth enveloping her as if the entire world has come to witness this precious, sacred union of souls reuniting.

She looked at Michael with sheer adoration. Time seems to slow down, and in that moment, she sees her past, present, and future intertwined with their cosmic union that transcends space and time. She reaches out to touch her heart in grateful recognition, and at that moment, she feels a profound connection not only to her divine counterpart, Michael but also to the deeper essence of their sacred love that resides in her heart. It is a radiant and illuminating path of their divine union with their shared gratitude and appreciation.

The love between Grace and Michael is a force of nature; it is a force that, when challenged, will always prevail; it is a potent blend of passion and affection that sets their hearts ablaze. As they finally stand face to face, ready to embark on this sacred journey together, the very air around them crackles with an unquenchable charge of what is Holy and sacred, a yearning that can only be sated by surrendering to their deepest desires within their sacred heart. With each passing moment, the intensity of their longing grows, the anticipation building to a crescendo that threatens to consume them both. Their bodies ache to be one, to taste the sweet ecstasy that awaits them in the embrace of their God-given holy divine union.

Their love, a divine spark of passionate bliss, emanates from their very beings, intertwining in a heavenly dance of holy love being confessed in the presence of GOD. An infinite love fuelled by divine urges that pulse within them, yearning to release their sparks of passionate love. Twin Flames are a pure and powerful expression of enduring love.

The marriage officiant begins the sacred ceremony, "We gather here today, bathed in the divine presence of GOD, to bear witness to the sacred union of Grace and Michael. Marriage is a profound symbol of the merging of two souls, reuniting in perfect harmony as one. It is a union that, far from diminishing, enhances the individuality of each partner. You see, my beloved, the beauty of this sacred bond lies in the recognition that you do not cast aside your unique essence, for it is precisely this essence that brought you together with such magnetic force. Marriage, then, becomes a tender proclamation, a declaration of love that resonates deep within your hearts, affirming that you shall forever embrace and cherish your authentic selves.

The relationship and each individual are continually growing and developing. Your understanding of each other deepens and evolves. It is not this ceremony or the state of being married that will truly join and hold you together; it will be your ongoing commitment to your relationship and to the kind of unity you wish to be together. In this way, your marriage will not be just a symbol; it will be more than that. It will be an action, something you work actively on every day.

You will find strength in knowing you have a true friend who will remain loyal and faithful to the end, forsaking all others."

The groom would like to say a few personal words to his Bride...

"Grace, we have been blessed with a great love. There was a feeling of inevitability when we met on the dance floor, and our lives were fated to converge like a cosmic dance.

I love everything about you, Grace; you truly are Amazing. I love your warm, caring heart for others; I love your courage, Your compassion, and your sincerity. I am in love with your flaming self-respect, and it's these things that I see in you that are admirable and exciting to me.

We didn't fall in love. We danced into love with our eyes wide open, and I want to dance through eternity with you. I would choose you in any version of reality; you truly are my one and only.

I pledge to you, my wife, devoted love, loyalty, integrity, and faithfulness within our divine union. You are my forever, my love, and I am eternally grateful to have you by my side."

The bride would like to say a few personal words to her Groom...

I love you so much with my whole heart, Michael, with a passion that can't be expressed in words, only in kisses, glances, and years of adventures together.

I promise to be your honest, faithful, and loving wife for the rest of my days. I love you more than any metaphor can ever try to express—my love, my husband. I will absolutely dance with you through eternity by the rhythm of our shared sacred heart and soul.

My husband, I invite you to share my life. You are the most loving, clever, and kind individual I have ever known, and I promise to always be in your corner. Together, I know we can do anything. I can't wait to work hand in hand to build a beautiful life and to achieve a healed and happy world together."

As the marriage officiant gracefully accepts the rings and continues, "Let us appreciate the depth of the ring's symbolism. Wedding bands, with their perfect circles, symbolize an eternal bond without a beginning or an end. However, we must acknowledge the truth that these rings do indeed have a humble origin. Rocks are excavated from the depths of the earth, while metals are transformed through intense heat, turning into liquid before being meticulously moulded, cooled, and painstakingly polished. Like these rings, love itself emerges from modest origins crafted by perfectly imperfect beings. It is a process that gives rise to something truly magnificent, where beauty is born from the raw elements of our hearts, turning what was once nothing into an extraordinary force of connection."

Bride and Groom repeat during ring exchange:

"With this ring is my promise to accept and love all that makes you "**You**". I promise my love will forever be unconditional and eternal."

The marriage officiant continues, "The couple will light the unity candle with their individual candles to symbolize their coming together as one." As they light the unity candle, a blessing is being given to the newlyweds: "Rejoice in your love for each other! GOD bless this marriage, and may your love for each other continue to grow. May GOD bless the two of you abundantly in the purity and innocence of love, joy, and happiness.

I now pronounce you husband and wife. Michael, you may kiss your bride." A long, passionate, sizzling kiss it was, they embraced with gratitude and excitement. The guests expressed excitement for the newlyweds Grace and Michael.

The reception takes place in the palace's immaculate ballroom, where tables are adorned with gilded candelabras and overflowing with floral centrepieces that spill over the edges. A live orchestra performs under twinkling soft lights, creating an enchanting atmosphere as guests dine on a sumptuous feast prepared by a world-renowned chef. Michael makes a toast, "First, thank you for coming, and thank you to all who have made this day truly extraordinary. We've all had quite a day with dreams fulfilled and prayers answered. To my wife, Grace, this has truly been a profound and magical day where dreams came true, not just for ourselves but also for our friends and family. Having been supporting these dreams to create a more beautiful and happier world through your own vision and bringing to life the warmth in your heart unselfishly for the betterment of others. You truly are Amazing Grace." raising his glass, "To my wife!"

Grace, with her radiant smile and flowing joyful tears, is moved by Michael's kind and loving words. Michael took her by the hand, "Grace, I would be honoured if you would join me for our first dance together as my wife and I officially as your husband." It was an eternal dance that began beyond heaven's gate, where everything is possible.

Twin Flames share an unbreakable, unconditional love for each other. It is the cosmic dance of two souls reuniting as one with a grand purpose to create heaven on earth. They are the pure holiness of GOD, eternal love, and infinite power to free others by this example of the purest love formed, and they are pillars of light for GOD manifested through their divine union, Free to love fully.

# Conclusion

In conclusion, the eternal dance of Twin Flame love is a divine connection that goes beyond the realms of ordinary passion. Twin Flames are two souls split from the same energetic flame, destined to reunite on Earth to fulfil a sacred purpose.

Their relationship is a unique blend of intense love, spiritual growth, and profound transformation. When Twin Flames come together, they ignite a powerful energy that transcends physical desires. They embark on a journey of self-discovery, unlocking the hidden depths of their souls and pushing each other toward spiritual evolution.

The purpose of Twin Flames is to bring heaven to earth—to create a harmonious balance of divine love in the physical realm. Their union serves as a catalyst for personal and collective healing, inspiring others to awaken to their own spiritual potential.

However, the path of Twin Flames is not without challenges. Their connection often triggers intense emotions, tests their resilience, and pushes them to confront their deepest fears. Through these trials, they learn the art of surrender, forgiveness, and unconditional love.

Ultimately, Twin Flame love is a sacred dance of transformation, where two souls come together to create a heaven on earth. They are bound by an unbreakable bond, guided by a higher purpose, and driven by an intense yearning for spiritual union. Together, they uplift each other and inspire the world with their unique and transcendent example of unconditional, enduring love.

This connection is the Source GOD manifested; it's a holy, beautiful, eternal love.

The fictional characters in this story of an example of twin flame love were inspired by not just my own twin flame relationship but twin flame relationships in general, and the fact of the matter is this unconditional love between two parts of the same soul is real, created by Source GOD itself, and their purpose and mission are real. Their love for humanity is a passionate love, and together, they will do all they can to bring everything to light.

It was an honor and privilege to bring forth the awareness of such a sacred, holy love.

Love is the answer to everything, and Love will always be the answer. There cannot be any other way.

Be the love you would like to see in our world by doing what is fun and makes you happy and experience joy.